SEPARATION ANXIETY

Stories by
Daniel Coshnear

SEPARATION ANXIETY

Published by Unsolicited Press.
Printed in the United States of America.
First Edition.

People, places, and notions in these stories are from the author's imagination; any resemblance is purely coincidental.

Attention schools and businesses: for discounted copies on large orders, please contact the publisher directly.

For information contact:
Unsolicited Press
Portland, Oregon
www.unsolicitedpress.com
orders@unsolicitedpress.com
619-354-8005

Cover Design: Valerie Coshnear
Editor: Robin Ann Lee

ISBN: 978-1-950730-65-0

The sensation is reverberative and seems to attach itself as the last link in a chain made up of all similar experience...there I was, buck naked, somewhere in the middle of the city and unwanted, remembering missed football tackles, lost fights, the contempt of strangers, the sound of laughter from behind shut doors.

The Fourth Alarm – John Cheever

There is no love that is not an echo.

– Theodor Adorno

Acknowledgements

hicksley.elizabeth(at)hotmail.com – *Fiction Attic Press*

Brooklyn Bound Q – *Pearl, forty-six, Fall 2012*

New Year's Resolutions Over Poker in the Back Room at the Comedy Club – *CSUF, DASH Journal, 11th Edition*

Echolalia – *580 Split,* Issue 5

The Donner Party – (Originally: Upon Return from a Family Vacation I Rent "*The Donner Party,*" a Film by Ric Burns) – *Oregon Literary Review Vol. 3 #2*

My Small Goals – *CUTBANK 83*

What Do You Want? – *Your Impossible Voice*

Above the Canyon – *Memoir Magazine, July 2018*

Where's Willoughby -- *The Cove,* an online magazine from Kelly's Cove Press

Rage, Rage – *BADLANDS Volume 8*

A Likely Story – *The Write Spot: Memories 4/19*

Proximity – *Gargoyle #71*

Eulogy for a Dead Comedian – *34th Parallel, Winter 2020*

An Ordinary Love Story – *Big Fiction Magazine, Fall 2019*

Thanks to friends and thoughtful readers: The editors at Unsolicited Press, Bart Schneider, Jennie Orvino, Harry and Linda Reid, Lyndsey Moore, Nancy Bourne, Lawrence, Richard, Valerie and Kimberly Coshnear. Special thanks to Valerie for the cover. Very special thanks to Robin Ann Lee and David Porter for reading my work with such care and scrutiny as if it were their own.

Contents

for Susan

hicksley.elizabeth(at)hotmail.com

Based on your Blockbuster rentals from November – December 2010, it's apparent that you enjoyed Keanu Reeves flicks (9), nearly as plain as you had some kind of a thing for Keanu Reeves, but there has been a spike since the new year in Fassbinder films, notably the 1969 classic, *Love is Colder Than Death*, and (6) others in (10) days. We don't know how to account for that change. Reaves – we decided – resembles your boyfriend (former boyfriend (?)) chin and eyes, and also your father, lips and nose, photos on Bing.

We also noted an 83% decrease in # of emails from you to your parents shortly after Xmas. Your bank activity did not change over the last quarter even with the expected rise preceding the holidays, but with the turn of 2011, or shortly before, we counted (8) transactions at site # CAD 0519, 174.6 miles from your nearest and most frequently visited ATM. Our records show (9) withdrawals from non-B of A ATMs, incurring fees of $13.50 since the new decade began. Coincident with the burst of withdrawals – $763.50 including fees – we noted a marked decrease in Costco purchases, particularly low-sodium Triscuits and low-fat Lucerne vanilla yogurt in the 12 pack, 8-ounce containers. We also found a marked increase in Martini & Rossi Sweet Vermouth from (0) to (2) 1.5-liter bottles, and over that same period from December 30 – January 11, we noticed another new preference Häagen-Dazs ice cream bars, coffee almond crunch, (3) four packs in 12 days.

Do you still buy toilet paper? Have you stopped feeding your cats? Library fees exceed $50, and your last attempt to borrow, *Everyman's Guide to Unsafe Mycelium*, was denied. Lucky for you, we say, but you bought a Mossberg 12 Gauge

Pump-Action Shotgun for $279.99. We also see you were billed full cost for a visit to Dr. Simon Lefkowitz mid-December, and we're quite sure you didn't go since at the time of your appointment, you purchased $36.19 worth of regular unleaded gasoline and a bag of spicy corn nuts 65 miles south of his office.

We are not contacting you now, in this case, to offer liposuction, Demerol, Cymbalta, or a weekend in the Bahamas. Although, on all of the above, we can guarantee a 20-30% savings until the end of January. We also have fantastic low rates of up to 50% on Wolfschmidt Vodka and the highest quality FMJ ammo. We write because we see you running headlong toward your own undoing, i.e. disaster, which is sometimes called immeasurable sorrow.

This – what you're in – is not a cave. This, dark as it seems, is only a tunnel. Your desires chart a course, and we know where you're going with a 3% margin of error. You might or might not ever love again, Beth. There's a limit to what our instruments can do. We think that perhaps regret is a bottomless vessel, but of this we are sure: there is no end of wanting.

Brooklyn Bound Q

She enters, takes a seat on the crowded bench opposite him, meets his gaze distractedly, and then peers into her handbag.

He looks down and then across the car to the left and the right of her. He lets his eyes roam and return to settle upon her glossy paperback. Is he brave enough to read the title? Sure, he is. He's interested in the book, in books, in what people are reading... Not in her.

She adjusts her glasses, scans the car quickly for another open seat as if to say, *I don't want your attention.*

He averts his eyes as if to say: *Don't flatter yourself.* Now, he's interested in footwear. He smiles approvingly at the feet, of an old man in purple high-top sneakers as if to say, *I have many interests. I value novelty, surprise, and risk.*

She is amused by her book, lets out a sigh and briefly smiles as if to say, *I don't even know you're here.*

The train stops. Two men in suits depart and two teens, a girl and a boy with backpacks and hoodies and baggy black denims shuffle into the space between him and her and take hold of the overhead railings. The teens commence a conversation.

"I read it," the boy says.

"All right. Who Nick?"

"He the one that telling the story."

"Who Daisy then?

"She the white chick that the other one is all hot for."

"All right. Who that other one and where he from?"

He looks up.

She looks up. She smiles briefly, as if to say, *I remember the book.* Or *I remember high school.* Or *Doesn't this seem ironic? These kids, in this time, speaking in those terms about that time.*

He smiles too as if to say, *Isn't the subway a magnificent experience?* Or *Isn't it better when we don't hide from one another?* As if to say, *you and I* – we – *are of the same background, the same class. We understand each other.*

The boy answers, "His name Jay. Just like my man, Jay Z."

"You don't know shit," the girl says.

He grins.

She grins.

The train stops, and the teens depart.

Her eyes revisit her book, dart back to him, and back again to the pages in front of her.

He permits his smile to linger and allows his gaze to settle on her, in an unfocused way, as if to say, *I'm at ease. I'm pleased. You're safe. I'm interested.*

She brushes her bangs with the back of her wrist as if to say, *I know you're watching.* As if to say, *I'm not uncomfortable.* As if to say, *I don't know what to say.* She closes her paperback, and with unusual care, she puts it back into her handbag. She is saying that her stop is next.

He bends to pull up his socks as if to say, *I didn't mean to embarrass you.* Or *Now you can look at me.* Or *This is my stop too. Maybe?*

She stands, turns to face the front of the train, turns her hips towards him, and pulls down the hem of her skirt. She looks down and up and back to the bench where she had been sitting. Then she finally risks a glance in his direction as if to say: *Are you going to follow me, you creep?* Or *It's now or never.* Or simply *Goodbye.*

He sets his hands on the bench beside him as if to steady himself for when the train slows down. Or perhaps to say, *I'm getting up. Give me a sign,* his face pleads. His eyes implore. *Eight and a half million people here, and I won't likely see you again. I'm not a creep, but...*

The train comes to a full stop. People exit; people enter. A crackling sound comes, and then a weary voice fills the car. "Next stop is Times Square. This is a Q train bound for Brooklyn. Change here for the N, R, S, 1, 2, 3, and 7 trains. Stand clear of the closing doors." As if to say, *Stand clear. The doors are closing.*

New Year's Resolutions Over Poker in the Back Room at the Comedy Club

It's your turn, Mitch.

What? I laid down two kings.

Your resolution, A-hole. Can't you pay attention?

New Years passed. Three hours ago.

You forgot your resolution already?

All right. All right. I'm going to drive slower through crosswalks...unless I see children.

Beautiful. That's beautiful.

Max?

I'm going to try to be more lactose tolerant.

I fucking wish you would. Whose turn is it?

I hate myself for saying this, but I love you guys.

Is that a resolution?

Next year, I'll love myself and hate you guys.

Ouch.

Ouch is right. Are you laying down a full fucking house?

I'm all in for world peace this year.

You said that last year, Leo.

How would you even know if the world was at peace?

I think I'd feel it.

What are you going to do to help achieve this world peace, Leo?

Ativan, I guess. Or better yet: *yoga*.

Weak.

Lame.

If I had to see you in yoga pants, that'd ruin my world peace.

What about you, B.D.?

You've been pretty quiet, B.D.?

It's called thinking, man. You should try it.

You've got our attention now, B.D.

I've got cancer.

That's funny?

What's funnier than cancer?

Testicular cancer. Enjoy that.

What cancer?

Ball cancer, idiot. My knackers are blowing up. My coin purse is overflowing.

That's a funny cancer, B.D. For real?

It's real.

Aw man.

Dude, what was that? Your mic-drop? End of show? Well I've got Ebola. And AIDS. And Eczema.

Shut up dude. He's serious.

For real, B.D? When did you find out?

Yesterday.

And you're here. What the hell are you doing here?

Where should he be?

I don't know… Some sad sack convention?

That's good, Leo. Can I use that?

You never asked before.

Well, I guess that's my resolution. I just thought of it. No more stealing. In general, I'm going to try to be a better human being.

I think he's shitting us.

Are you shitting us, B.D.?

Silence.

Guys, I'm going to need to borrow twenty bucks to stay in.

I don't lend money to guys with cancer. Nothing terminal. That's my bottom line.

Mitch, spot me a Jackson.

Wait. What stage are you in?

You're all pricks.

B.D. pulls a handkerchief from his pants pocket. It keeps coming and coming, red and blue and green and yellow. Old-fashioned circus bullshit. He wipes his eyes and blows his nose.

The only thing worse than a clown is a dying clown.

Leo pushes his pile of chips over to B.D. Max does the same.

Aw shit.

I hate this game.

I hate this year already.

The others push their chips in front of B.D.

Taking an Uber, Max?

I'm blacklisted.

What? Flirting or puking?

Are they mutually exclusive? You call; I'll pay.

How you getting home B.D.?

Fucking limo. I love you guys!

Glasses are emptied. Coats donned, zipped, and buttoned. Scarves are wrapped. Hats are pulled low to cover the tops of ears.

Sorry B.D.

Sorry, pal.

It's cold out there. Snow blowing sideways. Go through the park.

Yeah, the park is beautiful in the snow.

Enjoy the ride, man.

Above the Canyon

In my late teens and early twenties, I'd been a hitchhiker, a freighthopper, a sleeper in unlocked parked cars and abandoned buildings, a dumpster diver, and sometimes a shoplifter. I needed little, owned almost nothing, and did not take care of what I *did* have. Sometimes on the side of a highway, I'd sing like Springsteen: *"I wish God would send me a sign / Send me something I'm afraid to lose."* A decade later, God complied.

On the day in question, it so happened, I was singing Woody Guthrie to my four-year-old daughter.

As I went walking, I saw a sign there
And on the sign, it said, "No Trespassing."
But on the other side, it didn't say nothing.
That side was made for you and me.

I found myself in my mid-thirties with a daughter. A daughter with pumpkin cheeks and wispy blond hair. She was not quite as tall as my waist. We trespassed plenty together. I wanted her to feel brave; to believe the world exists for her discovery. I wanted her to climb fences, literally and metaphorically. It was ironic how being reckless made me feel safe. I was, of course, trying to retrieve old patterns of thinking and feeling. With her help, I clawed my way back to something familiar.

It was the middle of a hot day in early fall. My girl and I ventured a mile and a half from home, up on Sweetwater Springs Road, to a hillside above an abandoned mine that was fenced off and presumably dangerous. Down below were trees and shadows; just beneath our feet, there were ochre rocks, dust, stubborn patches of thistle, and a surprise, a handmade grave. In place of a headstone was an old-fashioned faucet with rust stains lining the marble basin. Tacked beneath it was a simple placard, black paint on a graying redwood plank that read 'Sharon Ann Simmons' with the dates of her birth and death. Someone had placed stones in a circle, smooth round rocks from the coast, and among the rocks, memorabilia – Mardi Gras beads, plastic flowers, ticket stubs, and a toy unicorn with a purple tail – were scattered, blanched by sun and partially dissolved by rain. Looking closer, I could see that some of the rocks had been painted with nail polish: *I miss you baby girl. My heart. So young and beautiful. Sweet angel.* I checked the dates again and subtracted. She was not yet seven years old when she died.

The unusual grave, alone on a hillside, made the loss of her almost palpable, and deeply unsettling. I'd have preferred to move onto some new adventure, but my daughter, who had seemed either shy or bored when we arrived, became curious. Behind the faucet, she found a couple of dolls, teacups, and bracelets. She examined one of the dolls and then the other. "What is this, Dad?"

"A memorial for a girl who died." I read the name out loud.

My daughter repeated it. "Sharon Ann Simmons."

Neither my wife or I had stepped inside a church since we were children, and neither of us felt the need to teach our child the faith of our grandparents. Our daughter had never been to a funeral before. To my knowledge, our four-year-old girl knew nothing about death or how people show respect for those who've passed on. She put one of the bracelets on her wrist and asked, "Can I keep this one?"

Finders keepers had been my motto, but this time, I told her no. "These things were left for Sharon Ann from people who loved her," I said. It seemed evident that some people loved her very much.

"What happened to her?"

"I don't know."

"Where is she?"

"Buried, I guess. Maybe here."

She put the bracelet back in the spot where she had found it. She folded her hands and bowed her head. I didn't know where she could have seen such behavior before. "I love Sharon Ann Simmons," she said solemnly to herself.

I was touched. But puzzled. Was this an instinctual response? Where could this sudden show of reverence have come from?

I heard voices rising from the canyon. Though I liked to trespass, I didn't like to stay too long.

I beckoned my daughter back toward the gap in the fence where we had come in. She walked slowly, maintaining her grief posture. "Come on, honey," I said. "We need to get out of here." I helped her with the fence, freeing her shirtsleeve from a stray piece of barbed wire.

But she stopped; one foot in, and one foot out. "How did she die?"

"Really, I don't know."

"Can we come here again?" she asked. "Please?"

Would this be a formative experience? Perhaps it was her first real awareness of mortality. Human mortality, that is. She had seen racoons and squirrels crushed on the road before. She had seen one of her goldfish upside-down and bobbing, which was traumatic enough.

But this was different. How did I want her to feel about it? Was it something to be explored or passed over quickly? What should I do with my face, my voice? I appreciated my daughter's apparent respectfulness, but was she sad? Did I want her to feel sad? A girl died long before her rightful time. Hell yes, it was sad. I could have felt sad, but I felt frightened.

I didn't want to convey fear even though some may have been appropriate. For me, life without attachment – and the fear that comes with it – had been somewhat empty. To answer her question, the best I could manage was a question of my own. "Maybe, honey. Why do you want to come back?"

"Next time, can we bring a shovel?" she asked. "Can we dig her up?"

The Donner Party

I got a call on a Wednesday from my friend, Steve Einstein, who had rented a condo at Donner Ski Ranch. *One bedroom*, he said, *would be vacant.*

He was characteristically enthusiastic. Would we like to go? Saturday, Sunday, and return on MLK Jr. day? Him, his son, son's friend, and some others. They'd be skiing. We could rent skis, or we could sled.

I didn't know how to ski. My kids didn't know snow. I said yes, but then asked my wife if *yes* was a good choice. Her face puckered. She wouldn't be able to join us since she was on-call. She was a family nurse-practitioner at the Alianza Medical Clinic in Healdsburg. She frequently got calls from mothers with infants who had diarrhea, especially on holidays. I didn't speak Spanish, but I could offer advice for treatment of infant diarrhea in Spanish in my sleep.

On Thursday, my wife bought gloves and boots for the kids. On Friday, I bought two cheap plastic sleds. We packed. We took her car, because it was newer, better, bigger, and faster. Our chains were in a little black bag in the shed. Sliced turkey, rolls, a dozen tangelos, pretzels, water, hard candy, and gum. My son would either learn to keep his mittens on, or he wouldn't.

What did I know about the Donner Party? Probably as much or less than you. Some of them ate some of the others. They were headed west. We headed east. I grew up in Baltimore where we had snow, and we had something called snow days.

These days, sometimes I wonder if I really feel happiness. It seems so fleeting, so muted. When I hear laughter, my first thought is; *What could possibly be so funny*? *Is this depression, dysthymia*? I don't know, but if I need a happy memory, and often I do, nothing beats my mental picture of the yard outside my boyhood bedroom window. Everything blanketed in white. The radio voice listed Maryland county school closings.

We saw our first signs of snow by the side of I80 at 3,000 feet, oh twenty miles east of Auburn. My heart felt lighter, almost fluttering. My driving foot felt heavy. My daughter's friend had made her a CD of 80s pop songs. Both my daughter and son liked "We Are the Champions" by Queen, so we played it repeatedly.

I didn't know what the Reeds, the Graves, nor the Donners did for entertainment. Maybe they prayed or sang hymns. Ric Burns didn't delve into that aspect of their journey.

First, there was mud. Then snow. Axles broke. Oxen wearied and died. Tempers flared. By the way, they had no roads, no stores. They had a map, but it was bullshit, made by a prick named Hastings who had not yet made the journey through Donner Pass (which was not yet called Donner Pass of course).

In the car, I mused out loud about the word 'recreation.' Take sledding, for example, in what sense was that re-creation? What in the hell did that mean?

"I don't know, Dad," my twelve-year-old daughter said.

"Play the 'we will' song," said my six-year-old son.

But as I sat to collect my thoughts, it was the 're' part of the word that got me. There was nothing 're' about the Donners' journey. Everything was new. What need had they for simulated thrills? I imagined their days were a mix of hypervigilance and exhaustion. Maybe someone had a banjo. Or maybe they all thought about where their next meal was coming from, which was something my father used to say about the whining children in his backseat on long family car trips.

I could get excited about snow, the rare kind of quiet it brought, the way it smelled, the way it softened every edge... I could get excited about my kids' excitement. They were perfect ages for sledding, snowball fights, and building a fort together. Together was a theme. We were re-together-izing, miles away from homework, who set the table, and whose turn it was to clean the rat cage. For these couple of days, I would be Dad and Mom, which meant I might have an ounce of say-so. But even more, I could be a kid again. Call it re-anticipation.

For the Reeds, the Graves, and the Donners, snow meant slow death. They dug into crevices, built fires, and wasted away. Some ventured from their camps up to the summit to look for a rescue party coming from the west. Some of them couldn't bear to return and watch their loved ones die.

I had a hell of a time getting the chains around the rear tires of my wife's Nissan Sentra until much later when I realized they went on the front tires. I'd made an ill-advised drive down to Truckee for what? Tomato sauce, turkey burger, and a loaf of Safeway's idea of French bread.

I think I wanted some time alone with my son, because he had been shy in our cabin among our new weekend family, and because earlier in the day my daughter and I triumphantly skied the bunny slope six times while he practiced sliding down the carpeted stairs in his snow pants. He fell asleep on the drive.

On the way back, after I had given up on the damn chains, we entered the inching westbound traffic back up to Donner Pass. He was awake now, nibbling on a corn dog and telling me about a machine his good friend Ben from school had invented. Ben, the boy who misses so many school days because of leukemia, shots, and blood counts. Ben, the boy of limitless imagination and good cheer three weeks out of every month.

My son's inventions were often elaborate and designed to dispose of 'bad guys' in one way or another. Ben had some of these too, but the one my son described was, if I understood correctly, like a portable hole. A movable portal. I could set it anywhere and pass through it to somewhere else.

Blinking yellow lights spelled "Chain Control" and warned there'd be a check post ahead. Would we be ticketed or merely scolded? Maybe someone would help me with the damn chains. Maybe en-route we'd slide at 5 mph under the tires of a crawling semi, die a slow, stupid death. I wanted one of Ben's holes. In my mind, I traveled back to the condo and decided not to go to Truckee. I decided that my son and I were having better quality time reading dinosaur poems and eating cereal from the box.

In short, we survived. So, did about half the Donner Party. At the check post, the checker mistook my wife's car for a four-wheel drive and waved us on. I felt a mix of guilt and relief as I imagine the surviving Donners et al. did. I vowed to try the damn chains again as soon as we got off the highway.

Now safely home, I did what responsible writers are supposed to do. I tried to make some meaning of my experience. I looked up the word 'recreation.'

1) An activity engaged in for relaxation or amusement.

2) Literally to create something that once existed before or was believed to have existed but no longer survives.

The two definitions – as I saw it – were like two distant cousins. Perhaps like my ski weekend and the Donners' horrifying adventure. I could look long and hard for resemblances, but most likely I'd only strain my eyes. But this was the part of my essay in which I would attempt to synthesize themes and shine a bright, golden light on some meaningful, transformative moment.

Here was where it all came together, or not.

I watched my kids marvel at icicles in a parking lot, and it bored me. Yes, I could remember. Yes, I was touched by their innocence and wonder. Yes, I was satisfied that I could show them this. But come on! How long was that supposed to last? Get back in the car already!

And yes, the fear of sliding under a truck had made me fully present, a sensation comparable to having my hair pulled out of my chest. For about five minutes. That got boring too.

I invented that little story about Ben's moving portal. In fact, I was too preoccupied to listen to my son at the time. I'd once seen a hole like the one described in a Bugs Bunny episode. Ben often tells me about his inventions when I drop my son off at kindergarten. He runs to me when I come through the door. His dark eyes shine. His descriptions are no more coherent than the recounting of a wild dream or an acid trip. I try to listen, but I always just stare at him. Or rather stare at the space around him as if I might see some trace of his spirit. As if his *joie de vivre* might somehow infect me or, pardon this Donners et al., nourish me.

My Small Goals

Monday

I dusted the light fixtures, deleted old emails, and put my pills in a plastic pill box. I washed dishes, dried them, and then set them in the cabinet. I peeled and chopped carrots into neat little sticks, a dozen per bundle. Three bundles. I made hummus from a recipe on the Internet. I read an article about celebrities with psoriasis. And another about how to make a fortune without leaving home. I did three sets of thirty crunches. Earlier in the day, I'd visited the clinic.

Dr. Fitzsimmons said, "It's anger turned inward."

Dr. Luongo said, "It's a loss of the sense self-efficacy, which means a loss of the feeling that you can get things done."

"Fundamentally," they said, "it's a loss of confidence."

"In what?" I asked.

"In yourself," Fitzsimmons said.

"In everything," Luongo said.

"What should I do?"

"You're doing it," Barbara, my nutritionist, said. "Eat well. Exercise. Rest. Watch the carbs."

"What else?"

"Don't drink, of course."

"Anything else?"

"Give the medication a chance to do its work," they said. "Don't worry. Set small goals for yourself, things you think you can achieve in a short period of time. Give yourself rewards for your accomplishments. We'll see you next week."

Tuesday

I pumped my bicycle tires to the regulation psi. I emptied the compost into a big bucket and carried that bucket to the back of the yard. I called to leave a message for Brenda re Todd's orthodontist appointment, but her answering machine was full.

I used to be the captain of a Special Weapons and Tactics (SWAT) Squad. The members called me Cap'n Crunch because I had a reputation for keeping cool under pressure.

I changed the vacuum cleaner bag. Well, there were some complications. The bag's cardboard opening was only three and a half centimeters in diameter, and the plastic tube which feeds into the bag measured four centimeters. The box of bags listed the brands of vacuum cleaners that *should* be compatible and an 800 number for support. I called and waited twenty-five minutes but never spoke to a customer service representative.

With a damp rag, I wiped Todd's soccer trophies until they sparkled. I polished the plaque in my office. *Chief Hostage Negotiator*, it says. It was given to me after my team successfully suppressed a riot at the state's supermax prison. There were no fatalities, not even an injury, except for the prisoner/hostage who had bitten off one of his fingers in the midst of a panic attack. I extracted the finger from the prisoner's clenched teeth, and within hours, a surgeon sewed it back on.

Wednesday

I called Brenda again, same result as yesterday.

I called the company that makes vacuum cleaner bags and waited ten minutes before connecting with Imamu in sales. He told me that it was raining in New Jersey, and that he had come from Nigeria where he had a wife and three daughters. I liked the music of his voice. I asked, and he told me his name means spiritual leader. Did he ever imagine he'd be selling vacuum cleaner bags for a living?

"No, sir," he said. He laughed. "I have never could imagine this life."

When he transferred me to customer service, I heard nothing but a high-pitched squeal. I completed the moderate Sudoku in the paper, and I read about a man who turned a weedwacker into a small propeller for his inflatable boat. I read advice for a woman whose husband denies he snores. I read about a university student who gunned down six classmates before shooting himself. No one saw it coming.

Once we leapt out of a helicopter onto the roof of a twenty-eight-story tenement. We were caught in the crossfire of rival gangs, and we army crawled to the nearest cover. Tim caught a bullet in the shoulder, near his heart. I caught one in my backside. It took four hours for our snipers to reach their proper coordinates and another thirty seconds to neutralize the assailants. I removed the bullet from Tim with a pair of needle-nose pliers sterilized in octane booster from my M249 machine gun. I flipped Todd's mattress and washed the sheets and pillowcases.

Before bed, I feasted on carrots and hummus.

Thursday

I heard a loud bang followed by a hissing sound around 2:46 a.m. Why was there orange smoke coming from my mailbox? Plumes of it? I felt it was Barry's idea. No, upon further thought, it had to have been Tim. Though Barry probably executed the plan with great enthusiasm. The crazy dumb fuck. I didn't miss the work, but sometimes I missed my team. I guessed that maybe they missed Cap'n Crunch too.

Unfortunately, a neighbor called the fire department. I told the crew manager to please step back, and he told me to please step back.

"Have it your way," I said.

He chopped the four by four post with his axe, and my mailbox tipped forward, spilling its contents onto the pavement: a fifth of Jim Beam (broken), a pack of Newport's 100's (my old brand), and a smoke grenade. The cigarettes were tempting. I put them in the glove compartment of my Nissan Sentra wagon, and while I was at it, I collected some of Todd's loose CDs and returned them to their proper cases.

On my way back to the house, I picked up a pressed log from the shed. I split it and fed a few pieces to the woodstove. A dark brown crust had formed on the surface of my hummus, but it was easy to remove with a spoon. I ate the celery that I had been saving in the crisper. Then I tiptoed back to bed. I lifted the quilt as gently as I could so as not...

But then I remembered. Brenda hasn't shared my bed in more than six months. Nights could be disorienting.

Thursday

I sat on the edge of my bed and rubbed my feet. They looked old and withered. I pretended my hands were not *my* hands. For a moment, I took some comfort in the caress.

I pushed myself toward the kitchen and pressed the button on the coffee maker, but apparently, I had forgotten to put any grounds in the filter. I watched the pot fill with water. *Anger turned inward?*

I took the bowl with the remaining hummus from my fridge and threw it at the sliding glass door, which lead to the deck. The glass door cracked but didn't shatter, leaving a lightning streak pattern like Neptune's trident. The bowl fell to the floor and sent up an ugly fountain of bean paste.

"How's that?" I hollered as if I weren't alone. "Now, I'm turning my anger outward!"

I felt little satisfaction from the gesture. I went back to bed.

Friday

At noon, I made coffee and considered changing out of my robe.

There was a message from Brenda on the machine. "Todd's going to a dance tonight. Sorry, I forgot to tell you, honey. Afterwards, he'll spend the night at Phillip's. He'll see you next week. Or I should say two weeks because of the wrestling tournament in Livermore."

I had a feeling that I should feel something other than relief. And another feeling that was difficult to describe. Like terror but muted. Something like the time we tried to defuse a bomb at the high school gym and failed. Seconds before the explosion, we plunged into the swimming pool. I feared that one day, maybe soon, I'd forget what I should feel. What was normal.

Okay, I thought. *No point in running out to Safeway for groceries. No point in washing the partially dried hummus off the wall either.*

In the mess, I thought I saw the profile of a swan, slightly elongated. Or it looked like an upright vacuum cleaner with a curved handle. Or it could have been the figure of a man on his knees with his head bent in supplication.

Curiously, it was all of these things, but I only saw one at a time. As hard as I tried, I couldn't see the changes coming, which was to say I couldn't identify the moment of change or some activity of my mind which caused the man to turn into a swan or a vacuum. I don't know how long I sat there, staring.

Later, I called the 800 number. A voice said, "This is Gary. How can I help you?"

"I want Imamu," I said.

“Sure,” Gary said. “He's helping a customer. I'll have to put you on hold.”

I nodded which of course was useless over the phone.

“Are you there?” said Gary.

“I'm here,” I said. “I'm holding.”

Eulogy for a Dead Comedian

Max finds a place to stand in the second row. He turns his sullen eyes to the leaden sky and then scans faces as the crowd fills the seats. Tell me this, Mitch. How come Leo's giving the hesped?

B.D. wanted no rabbis. No priests. None of that–

Sure, but why Leo? The man never had a kind word for B.D. when he was alive. Once, he said if anyone deserves cancer in the balls–

Mitch shrugs. We all talk shit sometimes.

That's some heavy shit.

Did I tell you about the time Leo interrupted my set at The Pound to try out his new material? The goddamn show went viral. Next day, I was a household name.

You told me... Whose household? Where is it?

Leo said he might have me open for him on his next tour.

He hasn't toured in what...like three years?

The point is this: Leo still puts ass in seat, bread on table.

Crumb on floor.

If you say so, Max.

He puts the bounce in my step. The twinkle in my eye. That better? The stick in my craw. :

The son of a bitch has two HBO specials! As far as I'm concerned, he can say whatever he likes.

Sycophant.

Fuck you! *Pause.* What's a sycophant?

Max shakes his head.

I heard that he did the same for you buddy, but it wasn't your night.

Wasn't his night either. And sure as hell wasn't new material. *He turns, gives Mitch a slow examination from head to toe.* This here is about B.D. Don't you get it? This is B.D.'s day!

Meaning?

You'll see.

Long pause. I don't think heckling a eulogy is a thing, Max.

Why not? I've done weddings, bar mitzvahs, even did a first communion once.

**

An overcast fall afternoon, Beth Moses Cemetery, Long Island. Umbrellas like black mushrooms sprout from the soggy green lawn. Some stand, some wipe down their metal chairs and sit.

Leo Schotz arrives in a short black limo with a long black overcoat, a gray suit, and blue tie. He greets B.D.'s parents with a handshake and a slight bow. Then, he takes his place behind a podium with the same somber face he wears to start a show. One would expect him to wave off the applause. Don't get your hopes up, *he'd say. But, of course, there is no applause.*

Behind him, B.D lies. in a closed casket beneath a canopy. A year ago, he had been obese with a lazy eye and a huge, clownish mouth. He had a default smile which belied his deadpan delivery. But cancer made him angular and unrecognizable. Face scratching. Scab picking. B.D. did not go gently into the good night.

Leo takes a yarmulke out of his coat pocket and presses it onto his crown. He tilts his bald, pink pate toward the three dozen in attendance.

We're gathered here today.

Are we gathered here? Are we not gathered over there, Leo?

Coughs into his hand. We're gathered right here, Max.

Nice opening, Leo. You googled the standard eulogy. Filled in the blanks?

A woman whispers: Please be quiet.

Leo mutters: You should learn to play poker, my friend. It'd improve your disposition.

Is that what you think this is about?

You should show some respect.

I'm here to show respect!

Leo clears his throat. In a low, soft voice. Show me some respect, Max. *Louder.* Show some respect for Mr. and Mrs. Davidoff. *He nods to B.D.'s parents in the front row.*

Mrs. Davidoff stands as if on cue. Bogdan was not an easy child. Very stubborn.

Mr. Davidoff pulls her back down into her seat. Not now.

Leo offers his old, patented smile. His soft, brown eyes say that we're in this together. Can you imagine, showing respect is not our strongest suit?

She stands again. One of his high school teachers said to us, I don't mind a class clown if he's funny, but Bogdan is not funny.

High school teachers are a tough crowd, almost as tough as fellow comedians. *Leo shoots a look at Max and glances down at his papers.*

Tell us all about B.D., Leo.

Bogdan was an only child, born and raised in Brighton Beach.

Except for his sister.

Leo's smile turns rictus, possum-like.

It's not your fault, *says Mrs. Davidoff.* She died when he was two. He barely knew her.

Leo sighs, turning the page. Bogdan was an excellent student. A bright young man.

Mr. Davidoff timidly raises his hand. Excuse me. I don't mean to interrupt.

Why not? Join the party.

Well, you're half right.

Leo's voice rises. He graduated from Yale with a bachelor's in philosophy!

It was a community college, and he dropped out in his second semester.

He had a quarrel with a fellow called Aristotle, *says Mr. Davidoff.*

Max, laughing: You're on a roll, Leo, don't stop.

He was very intelligent, *says Mr. Davidoff.* I'll give you that.

Too much smarts, *says Mrs. Davidoff.* He thought he had a head for business. Remember the gefilte fish in a juice box?

I think that was a joke, *says Mr. Davidoff.*

What about Hookers with Hospitality? That was no joke.

Let's don't --

For any family occasion, *says Mrs. Davidoff.*

Let's not go there, *says Mr. Davidoff.*

A woman appears from behind a tree, negotiating her skinny pumps on the soft grass. She has on a miniskirt, fishnets. Her coal-black hair and spider-like eyelashes do not match her peach-colored freckles. She's wearing a face that seems incapable of surprise.

Mitch leans into Max, whispering. B.D.'s girlfriend?

You could call her that.

Was it a contractual thing?

Max straightens: It's good of her to show up.

It was good of her to gift him the clap too. That's what I heard.

What I heard, Mitch, is that he fucking loved her.

Not like you to get so emotional, my friend. Need a hankie?

Max reaches into his hip pocket and pulls out a handkerchief attached to a handkerchief attached to a handkerchief. Nine in all. Four feet long. Nah. I'm set.

That was B.D.'s! He gave it to you?

After his last show at The Armpit. He crushed it, and the goddamn seats were empty!

Woman's voice, louder whisper: Please be quiet!

Another voice follows: Ssshhh!

Leo clears his throat. I first met B.D. at a club in L.A. in 2005. We were all young then; we were all idiots. We'd blow through an hour's worth of material in ten minutes. Most of it was garbage: pratfalls, balloon animals, anything we could think of. But still… B.D. knew how to pause, to breathe. He wasn't afraid of silence… I learned a lot from him. I had never seen anyone hold the audience in his hands the way B.D. did.

Guess I heard it different.

Leo mumbles. Don't know what you heard, Max.

Guess I heard you say that the only part of stand-up comedy B.D. understood was the standing up part.

It could be my thinking has evolved since then.

Could be the opposite.

Nice retort, buddy. You'd be a hit in the schoolyard. The preschool yard. *Leo touches his brow with his coat's sleeve.*

Could be that you never showed up at one of B.D.'s gigs.

Maybe I had my own career to think about. Maybe you should try it.

Could be that you never showed at Mercy General when B.D. was in his darkest hours. It could be that he asked about you every time I saw him. He worshipped you, Leo. But you–

A long pause. A low voice. I don't like hospitals.

Well that's where were we differ then, I guess. I love hospitals. When I'm looking for a good time, my first choice is always oncology.

Leo looks at Mitch, pleading.

Mitch leans towards Max. Cool it, huh?

Necrosis. Ulcerating tumors. They give the air a fresh, spring-like scent. *Max closes his eyes and inhales.* But if I'm being honest, it's the children's weeping and wailing in the wee hours. Pure symphony.

You don't know what Leo has been through.

What have you been through, Leo? Wait. Don't tell me. Hardship? Is that the word you're looking for, Mitch? I hear he's been collecting vintage cars.

The girlfriend had found a seat in the back row, but now she stands up. How does this work? Can I say something?

Leo grunts: Be my guest.

I saw you in the lobby, Mr. Schotz. It wasn't easy to tell that it was you with the hat and sunglasses. I guess being famous has its drawbacks, you know... I get it though. There are a lot of times, you know, when I want to be invisible.

Mrs. Davidoff leans towards Mr. Davidoff. Not likely in that outfit.

Leo's eyes swim before returning to the paper in front of him, an old review from the New York Post. B.D. is truly one of a kind. His act mixes performance art and stand-up. He promises to make a rabbit appear from a hat, but most of his fifteen-minute routine is spent looking for the hat among bags and boxes. Sometimes, it seems as if he is talking to himself, a litany of miseries: disappearance of his wife, separation from his children, loss of his beloved dog (sleeping on the neighbor's front porch), and loss of his career right before our eyes. The act is interrupted by a phone call, presumably from his ex, in which he assures the delivery of child support and pleads for time. One could find shades of Shandling, Kaufman, and even Dangerfield, the man who got no respect, but the most apt comparison I can make is to an old-fashioned circus clown. B.D. made me want to laugh and cry at the same time.

Where'd you get that piece, Leo? B.D. hasn't done the magic bit in five years. Tell me, what did he do in his last show?

I didn't –

Of course, you didn't.

What did he do, Max?

He was a self-narrating mime.

Leo pounds a fist on the podium. I didn't want to do this…this…whatever! B.D. called me. He texted me. He *begged* me. Why me? I don't… I don't know!

He grimaces at the front row takes a deep breath and continues in a more plaintive tone. We're here to remember B.D. Are we not here to remember B.D.?

You stood in front of the elevator door, Mr. Schotz. Frozen. I could have gone up with you, you know. I would have held your hand.

Leo swigs from a bottle of water. I don't believe I ever met you.

My name's Candy… Candy Beaver.

Scattered chuckles.

Clueless parents, *she says.* Hey, B.D. had something he wanted me to share with you.

Perhaps after–

Candy seems not to hear. Or not to care. Or rather it's as if it never occurred to her to ask for permission. She makes her way up the short aisle to the podium, flips open the flap on her shoulder bag and takes out a cylindrical package wrapped in tissue, tied with a ribbon. She turns and says. Hi Mr. and Mrs. D.

Leo promptly slips the package into the pocket of his overcoat.

Max: Whoa! Not so fast. What is it?

Mitch: I must admit, Leo, I'm curious too.

Leo casts a suspicious look at Candy. He sighs, digs the package out of his pocket, and fusses briefly with the ribbon. The rain, which had been threatening all day, lets loose upon the umbrellas, explodes upon the asphalt and the hoods of cars one hundred feet away. The wind blows the tops of a pair of pitch pine together, presses coattails to the backs of trousers, dresses into nylons. A woman's black hat lifts and tumbles until it rests against a headstone. For a moment, the canvas canopy above the coffin fills and looks as if it might launch. With another gust of wind, it flattens.

Max: I think B.D. wants you to open it.

Leo looks spooked. He shoves the package back into his coat pocket. Zay Gezunt, *he says.*

Can you believe this guy? What? Have you lost your sense of humor, Leo? Where are you going?

**

Twenty minutes pass. Enough time for Leo to pull his long, black overcoat across his chest and storm off towards his limo to sit, smoke, and try to collect himself.

Time for an old gentleman, perhaps a representative of Beth Moses, to step to the front and offer a brief prayer in Hebrew.

The Davidoffs, with furrowed brows, exit arm in arm as quickly as their old bones can carry them.

Mrs. D: Nothing will surprise me ever again.

Mr. D: I did not see that coming.

Max and Mitch hit pause on their volley of insults to have their picture taken by a reporter from one of the tabloids. Mitch hesitates by Leo's limo but can't quite bring himself to tap on the tinted glass.

Last view of Max: driving off in his wife's Fiesta sedan with the window opened wide as he wipes the windshield with a rag.

The crowd has departed, all but one. Candy sits alone in what has become again a light drizzle. She stands and weaves toward the road. Could be the heels. Could be the fact she's high as a kite. Maybe she is heavy-hearted in an unbalanced way. As she approaches the road, the limo's rear window descends and a sweet, skunky cloud escapes.

Thanks for nothing.

It takes her a moment to register where the voice has come from. Can I get a hit of that?

Leo opens the door and steps out. He pushes the joint at her.

She takes a long pull. Then another.

Gruffly and disinterestedly. How'd you meet B.D.?

He was in the market for a blowjob.

Oh.

I don't usually get friendly with clients.

Clients?

Later, you know, I'd see him on the ward. B.D. was kind. Generous.

I should say so! *Leo takes the unwrapped package out of his pocket and slams it down on the roof of the car. It's a glass jar filled with a brownish, reddish liquid, the color of a diluted Manhattan. Suspended in the solution are two murky things; one is the size of an apricot, and the other is the size of a grape.* He gave me his goddamn gonads! Who does that?

B.D. does that. *A look of puzzled concentration.* And maybe the guy behind the curtain.

What?

From that old movie.

What? The Wizard of Oz? *Leo's face contracts as if he has encountered some awful smell.* Well, I didn't ask for them. I don't want them!

Candy removes her black wig and reveals her pale scalp, which is bald except for a scraggly tuft of hair on the back of her head. B.D. bought me this one. It doesn't really match my complexion. *She replaces the wig with another from her handbag, platinum blonde.* Thanks for the smoke, Mr. Schotz. I'd better be on my way.

Leo settles back into his limousine and presses his joint into the ashtray. Five seconds later, he is out again, chasing Candy across the wet lawn. Hey!

Candy turns, rests one hand on the nearest headstone.

I used to have friends. I used to enjoy what I do.

She fixes her wig into place.

B.D. must've really hated me, huh?

Her tone is nearly as flat as her affect. The man was unfair, but, you know, he was right about one thing.

Max? That prick?

He said B.D. worshipped you.

Bullshit.

He watched all your performances, and every talk show. The radio shows even. You know, he had bootlegs of old bits from clubs that don't exist anymore.

So, then why–

Candy shrugs.

Why?!

He said you had a gift. You knew how to look at things sideways. Then, you just stopped looking. He said success had… That you had lost your –

Balls? Christ!

He said you could have been as good as Carlin.

Carlin? I don't believe it.

A smile faint like a cloud shadow plays across Candy's face. Do you know which was his favorite show?

Surprise me.

Charleston, Virginia. The time you got booed off the stage.

Not surprised.

Candy holds up one fist like it's a microphone. She tilts her head, looks up into the darkening sky with a quizzical expression. We're coming to the end of Black History Month. Soon, it'll be Women's History Month. Can we just, for god sakes, hear it for the men in the room? Go ahead. Give yourselves a hand. *She counts three beats.* No, I'm sorry. I meant the white men. *She counts three more beats.* No, I'm sorry sir. Just the straight white men. *She counts three more beats.* You sorry bastards. Do you really think you need recognition?

Leo's mouth is wide open. How many times can he be stunned in one day?

I guess it played better in San Francisco.

When Leo laughs his shoulders drop two inches.

Candy turns and walks.

You're soaking wet. You must be cold.

She walks on.

Can I offer you a ride somewhere?

She stops, casts her gaze around the cemetery. There's not another car in sight.

Hey. I promise no funny business.

Funny business, you know, is the least of my worries from you, Mr. Schotz.

At this, Leo's eyes go wide. He clutches his chest and falls to one knee. Candy watches blank as a paper plate until he pitches forward into a puddle. He pushes himself up. Mud streaks across his face.

You've ruined your suit, Mr. Schotz. *She emits a girlish chuckle.* Maybe there's hope for you yet.

Echolalia

Edwin was naked, laughing, loping up the stairs. Crapping as he went. Alicia, said, "Get out of here. I'll take care of it." She already had a plastic bucket of Clorox II and a rubber glove from a previous mess. I departed the West Fourth Street House quickly. I was grateful for Alicia, but I left without directions or petty cash.

The year was 1985, and I was escorting five of the ten residents – George, Nikki, Joey, Peter and Yvette – to a birthday party at another Association for the Mentally Retarded (AMR) group home somewhere near the Broadway/East New York subway station. It was a forty-minute ride from Greenwich Village to a part of Brooklyn that I had never been to. I knew the area was poor. Two months ago, three or four men broke into the intermediate care facility, robbed them, and beat the staff on duty. Rumor had it the staff pissed blood and was hospitalized. AMR admin kept quiet on the subject because of a lawsuit.

One. Two. Three. Four... Where the hell was Joey? Five. I made six as we descended into the dark station. "Twelve tokens and a receipt, please." The token salesman shook his head. He could say or do whatever he wished behind the half-inch thick glass. He didn't wish to write me a receipt. He didn't want to explain.

Keynotes from our last staff meeting:

1) We must try to help our clients blend in with the community.

2) We must get receipts for any expenditures on clients' behalf.

3) If you fail to get a receipt, you will *not* be reimbursed.

The cost of our excursion was equal to what I was going to get paid for it, give or take a couple bucks. But I wasn't doing it for the money; that was not part of my confusion.

People told me that I looked like Vincent Van Gogh (or more likely the actor who played him in the popular *Vincent).* I think some may have mistaken my inwardness for some secret burning intensity. In fact, I often didn't know what I wanted. I had been a philosophy student at NYU, but I dropped out to discover myself. To discover not-myself really. To uncover the rational underpinnings for our empirically based systems of belief. Um no. I thumbed an Etch A Sketch pattern across the country until I was broke and thoroughly lost before I returned to Greenwich Village eleven months later for the same reason I'd left: Celia.

Like me, George, Joey, and Peter were single young men. They seemed to know what they wanted though.

Joey wanted to go to the circus. He wanted to be Batman & Robin for Halloween. He wanted his parents to visit every day, but they came only once a month, and on those visits, he needed to be coaxed out of his closet. I could relate.

Peter wanted to lie in bed and play with his genitals. He wanted ice cream whenever he could get it. If he was awake, one could be sure he was grinning. Sometimes his grin was so wide that it appeared to curl his entire face. I despised and admired Peter.

George wanted what Peter wanted when he was with Peter, what Joey wanted when he was with Joey, etc. In addition to severe mental retardation and schizophrenia, George had a condition called echolalia. He often repeated what had been said to him, particularly when he was nervous or eager to be friendly (which were hard to distinguish).

Yvette wanted to be told her hair looks pretty. She purred. She didn't have any words, but with shrillness, she could make her likes and dislikes known. She didn't like to be touched.

Nikki, on the other hand, could be plainspoken. Sometimes, she'd say, "I want a man to lick my pussy." She was a heavyset, black woman of twenty-five years. Her ass followed her like a dog on a leash. She had high cheeks. She had stunning eyes, especially when a strange man showed her attention. When she applied makeup, as she did for the day's adventure, her lovely brown complexion glowed florescent pink and orange. One of Nikki's goals – one of the *program's* goals for Nikki – was to accept staff's help when applying makeup.

Rattle and screech. Our train arrived. One. Two. Three. Four. Five. And I made six. No one stood. Bench seats were available in the center and each of the far corners of our car.

I was wearing my new secondhand, black leather jacket and Converse red high tops. I felt pretty hip. I hadn't called Celia since I had returned to New York, because my hipness hadn't solidified yet. Because I thought I may have learned something, but I didn't know what. Because I was afraid. We might meet again exactly where we had left off. She might not have missed me at all. She might have found someone else.

Regarding *blending in*, it was my job to try not to look like a group leader. I was to pretend we were not a group, though of course my ass would be written up if I lost any of our members, and I'd likely lose my job. I wished Nikki would not have chosen to sit so far away. George followed her. I stayed close to Joey, because he had been known to bolt. Yvette sat by me.

"Your hair looks pretty, Yvette," I said.

Peter sat on the opposite side of Yvette. "Ice cream?" he asked in his high, chirping voice.

"We'll see."

"Hair ugly," he said. He leaned forward and gave me a patented grin.

"Cut it out."

"Nuh! Nuh!" Yvette said. She had only one volume: fully cranked. A handsome woman sitting opposite of us looked up from her paperback. A pair of teen age girls whispered in Spanish, and one laughed out loud.

"Hair ugly," Peter said.

"I'll give you knuckle flavored ice cream," I said as quietly as I could.

The subject of intelligence intrigued me when I was a student. It confounded me on the job where my closest relationships were with severely retarded men and women. For what it mattered, Nikki scored in the high forties on her IQ test, Joey and Peter scored thirty, and Yvette and George scored in the mid-twenties.

Gilbert Ryle, a philosopher, made a distinction between *knowing that* and *knowing how*. None of the residents of West Fourth Street House, except perhaps Nikki, could have told me *that* New York City was in New York State or *that* New York State was in the United States. But each, except perhaps George, knew *how* to get his or her needs met. Wittgenstein, roughly paraphrased, said intelligence equals proficiency in a language game – *but there are innumerable language games.*

"Hair ugly," Peter said. He studied me. His odd brain was working at full capacity.

"Nuh! Nuh!" Yvette said.

"Ice cream down your back," I said.

Again, the woman looked up from her glossy novel with a disapproving glare. So often I lost at games. *The meaning of a word or phrase is its use in a language game. Meaning equals use. Use is defined by context.* I could say these things, but did I comprehend them? Only fleetingly. I got glimpses but never solid footing. I understood that Peter was not playing for one bowl of ice cream. He was investing in an ice cream future. At the West Fourth Street House, they called it *testing*. "You're new," I was told. "Expect Peter to test you."

Before we left the house, I tried to intervene in Nikki's makeup process. "Just a touch of that looks nice," I said in accord with the behavioral methodology. My prompt might have been better received had not another staff already intervened.

"Fuck you, asshole man," Nikki said.

I didn't trust my pull with Peter. What would happen on the ride home after the promised ice cream bowl had been consumed? I trusted my power to persuade Nikki even less. I wished I hadn't snapped back when she rebuffed me.

"Are you trying to look retarded?" I asked. With a bit more patience, I might have convinced her to wear a skirt that covered her crotch when she sat.

We stopped at our final stop in Manhattan and came to the long flickering ride under the East River. I remembered Celia as I often did in a moment's quiet – the conspiratorial smile, the time I unzipped her dress, and kissed her neck. She turned, put her soft mouth on mine. We were in her dorm room at NYU, just back from a party at another dorm. The sweet smell of pot smoke in her hair.

"I think I love you, Kenny," she said.

"I think I love you too."

Enter Brooklyn and two young black men dressed in black with flourishes of silver and gold. One with a hood pulled so far down that it covered his eyes. The other with a cane but no apparent limp. They sat opposite Nikki and George, about twenty feet from where I sat. Nikki gave the man with the cane her stunned look. I think it was meant to say, "I want a man to lick my pussy." Her inadequate skirt said the same. She looked at me briefly. So did the men. I did not feel hip. I felt white, proprietary, and scared.

"Your hair looks pretty, Yvette," I whispered.

"Hair ugly," Peter said.

I was thinking that I had been tested plenty at NYU. All my life, I had been predisposed to search, to try to see behind the world of the everyday for the true order. The axiomatic. I saw experience like a tent rippling in the wind and laws like a frame, supporting it. Meaning was a map, and I only needed to discover the legend. I believed in Leibniz and Spinoza, and I cherished the *Tractatus Logicos Philosophicus* of Wittgenstein, but soon enough, I was challenged by his later philosophy – the dismantling of his early work – all those curious snapshots which could neither be indexed nor cataloged. And I was broken by the simple semiotics of love.

There had been another party. A different dorm. A stranger's room. I was jealous and confused. My mind ached with contradictions.

"Let's go. I'm tired," I said.

"You go," Celia said. "I'm having fun."

I heard George's high-pitched voice first at the far end of the train car. He was either nervous or wanted to make friends. Or both. I couldn't make out the words. My furtive glances in his direction were not fooling anyone.

"Where you going all dressed up?" the man with the cane asked Nikki.

"What's your fucking problem?" the man with the hood asked George.

"Fugging problem?"

Nikki spoke slowly through a big smile like she was high on nitrous oxide. "We're going to par-tee."

"Hair ugly," said Peter on the bench beside me.

"Nuh!" Yvette flounced herself onto the bench across from us, where the handsome woman had been sitting, before she had moved to a different car.

"Circus?" Joey asked.

"Nikki." I waved at her. "Why don't you come and join us?"

She waved back at me, smiled. But didn't move.

"Where you going?" Nikki asked the men across from her.

"We're going to par-tee," Cane mimicked. The two men laughed. Nikki rocked backward then forward in silent, breathless laughter.

George laughed. I was trying to remember if he had gotten his Phenobarbital before we left.

"What's so funny?" Hood asked George.

"So funny." George laughed again like the sound of a fork in a garbage disposal.

"Fuck you," Hood said.

I stood. I tried not to think. The sway of the train was not gentle. Every step felt uncertain like the time I sampled George's Haldol and found that I couldn't walk more than ten steps without having to stop and massage my thighs and calves.

Like the time I dropped to my knees before Celia. It was nighttime in Washington Square Park. A block from her dorm. The last of the parties had ended, and the sleepless city was tucking itself in. It was December. The ground was wet and cold. We had been arguing, but I don't remember how it started.

"You need to loosen up," Celia said. "I think I don't love you, Kenny." She held her lipstick tube between us, a single post in an impossible fence. "Love is a feeling. Sometimes I feel it, and sometimes I don't."

"Words are shadows then, transitory. Promises are mere exclamations of feeling."

I tried holding onto the overhead rail, but it made me feel big and false like a frightened animal puffing up. Too committed. Too much of a target. I let the railing go, and the train's thrust jerked me back too quickly to the foursome.

George's pronunciation was unusually clear. "Fuck you."

Hood rose to his feet.

George stood. He extended his hand to shake.

"Hey man." I said, searching for light under the hood. I felt the cane pressed against the crotch of my pants. "He doesn't get it. He doesn't really want–"

"That's just George," Nikki interrupted. "And George is cra-zee." She illustrated with a rotating finger beside her head.

"Cra-zee?" George asked.

"And who the fuck is this?" Cane asked Nikki.

"He with us," said Nikki. "He asshole man."

Cane laughed and bumped fists with Hood, who didn't laugh.

"Why don't you tell asshole man to mind his own business," Hood said.

Hood shoved George, and George fell back into his seat.

My breath dropped out of my lungs.

George bounced back, pressed his belly against Hood's. "Fuck you?"

Behind me, at the opposite end of the car, I heard a whoosh and rattling of the wheels on the metal tracks. The door opened and closed with a clack. Someone was coming. Something had changed. But I was afraid to turn my head.

"Whyn't you come with us," Cane said to Nikki. "We'll show you a bad time."

She smiled and attempted to cross her enormous legs. Her head rolled back on her shoulders. What I saw was the dripping basement of an abandoned tenement, a girl on her hands and thick haunches. Crying. A broken bottle pressed to her throat. There had been such a story in the news only a week before, a gang rape in Flatbush. Her eyes found me briefly, and I saw what I thought was a flash of fear, almost surely a reflection of the fear on my face.

"Nikki?"

"Fuck off," Cane said. The tip of his cane moved to my stomach.

"Nikki please! I didn't mean what I said to you back at the house." I knelt to meet her gaze as the cane pressed against my throat. "I didn't mean it. I didn't."

She was often slow to speak, but in that dreadful moment, I traveled. I was eleven months lost only to surface in lower Upper Sandusky, a few from miles from Massillon. Factory flame and the taste of rubber. West of Lincoln and east of Brush, hay swirling off the back of a speeding eighteen-wheeler. East of East St. Louis and south of East L.A. Weeds in the cracked asphalt. Dogs signing fences. Not far from Fargo, pickups with rifle racks. *Ass, grass, or gas; nobody rides for free.*

It was always an hour past twilight. The highways were too wide. Lights too small, too yellow. I was broke and shivering in downtown Denver, ten minutes late for dinner and my cot at the Jesus Saves Mission. No government surplus chili. No moldy bun. No rest. No clue why I wouldn't – or really couldn't – call my parents, or a friend, or Celia, except that to call for help would translate all my suffering into defeat. Mere helpless hardship. And this... This single belief that I was the captain of my ship, however aimless the journey. A route would reveal itself. A map for me.

"I didn't mean it, Nikki. I didn't. I'm so, so sorry."

And upon saying so, I was back at the Denver bus station, a minute before midnight. A blue uniform with a stick tapping the plastic chair under my ear. "Got a ticket?" Then "Gotta go."

I leaned toward the door and out toward the brightest lights in the burning cold. A marquee. The shining faces of smartly groomed rock 'n' roll fans filtered through velvet ropes to shining cars. I heard a bubbling laugh and saw a smile that stabbed me with the memory of Celia. The lights got dimmer, and streets turned into alleys. Broken fences. Shapeless lots. My anger towards that blue uniform with his stupid-ass black shades kept me warm for an hour. But the night was long, and with the darkness, came the chill, exhaustion, and fear soon enough. With that fear came the footsteps. *The ones I had thought were my own*. The overtaking shadows. The horrible discovery I had made the day I set off and every day thereafter. I was defenseless when I was out of context, kicked in the back until I bled. Bottle blade at the throat. I would disintegrate if I was no one to anyone. *Is this what I came to tell you, Celia? I am so not ready.*

"Nikki." I swallowed hard. "Do you have any – *any* –idea how beautiful you are to me?"

Again, her head rolled back. Silent laughter. The cane's tip raised a slow inch until it pressed against the top of my Adam's Apple. *Words are only expressions of feeling.* My mind replayed the scene: Celia Walking Away from Me. The time I snatched her hand in mine. "You need to loosen up," she said. "I think I don't love you."

"Love is love!" I spun her, so we were facing each other. Such a pouty, sulky look like I had never seen. Maybe her father or mother had grabbed her hand, spun her, and demanded her attention in that way before. I could see that it wasn't working, but I persisted. "Love is not a mood. Love is not merely the time of day!"

"You can't–" She pulled her hand back and walked away.

"You're a spoiled bitch."

She passed between parked cars and into the street. Hips. Hair. Swinging purse. She turned the corner and was gone.

"Nikki! Nikki!" My throat was full. She was a blur through my tears. "I'm crazy for you."

"You crazy all right," she said.

"You're my girl, Nikki. Be my girl."

She showed the men 'crazy' again with her rotating finger. She laughed her breathless laugh but then said, "He not too bad. He okay."

"You one crazy bitch," Cane said. He looked past me to the other end of the car. Something *had* changed. A sudden pressure drop. "Sometimes I like a crazy bitch," he said, "but you're too crazy." Cane rose to his feet.

Hood rose too, taking a long second to stare witless George down. The two brushed by me and stood beside the nearest door.

Nikki swayed toward the rest of our group in the center of the car. George ran, sliding into the space next to Peter. "Hair ugly?"

"Fuck you," Hood said to me as the train came to a stop.

"Fuck me," I said to his back through the open doors. I breathed.

I heard the hard tap of a wooden baton on the plastic seats. Then again on the chrome poles overhead. "Step aside," he said. He was a burly figure with a dozen devices waggling from his belt. He was the cause of these effects. Not me. I felt his gravity as he passed, and I thought it wasn't long ago that I thought I had some shit figured out.

But never mind that. I was on my knees again, Celia. I tried. I reached. I stretched. I fucking *loosened up.* Get this: I think I love you, and I think I don't love you too.

Separation Anxiety: A Light Romantic Tragedy

2/5/05, 9 a.m.

Dr. Donleavy looked at his watch, licked his right thumb, and flattened the thick black hairs on his left wrist. Lisa peered at Charlie over the top of her glasses, some mix of concern and annoyance. It was a handy expression in this line of work, and she used it often.

"You want to pursue this, Charlie?" Dr. Donleavy asked.

"Because I don't think it's a good idea," Lisa said.

Charlie felt perspiration collecting at the base of his spine, a single drop heading south. "Listen," he said. "Things get prickly with Dr. Leland, but that doesn't mean she should always get her way."

"Barbara always gets her way?" Dr. Donleavy pressed.

"What do you mean by prickly?" Lisa asked.

"Yes," Charlie said, "and you damn well know what prickly means."

"Let me get this straight," Dr. Donleavy said. "Dr. Leland scheduled her pre-orientation session for eleven in a small conference room at the Sulk Mental Health Center. Which was when and where you planned to meet with your residence supervisors. You're saying she wiped your initials off the dry erase board?"

Charlie nodded.

"Then I suppose we'll have a four-way," Lisa said. "If Dr. Leland… If Barbara…is willing."

"And if you're not satisfied," Dr. Donleavy added, "we know that you know where the grievance forms are."

They both promptly stood. When Charlie reached the door, Lisa said, "Charlie."

"What?"

"*Charlie.*" She shook her head.

"*What?*"

"How long have you been with us?"

"I was hired two weeks before you."

She shook her head again, wearily amused.

Dr. Donleavy laughed his trademark laugh. "Have an herbal tea, Charlie."

"Something soothing," Lisa added.

Consistent behavioral change is preceded by or concomitant with cognitive change (Liebowitz & Sulk 1997). Charlie almost believed that he could get over this bullshit with Dr. Leland. He could, for example, accept that he doesn't know who erased his initials. In the absence of verifiable information, his persistence only served to cast doubt on his already uncertain judgment. He knew that those who didn't think he was an asshole – which was to say those hired since last year's Christmas party – would soon start thinking so.

11 a.m.

"This is Sulk Hall, Charlie," Clare said. They had passed in the foyer as he was trying to intercept his residence supervisors, to spare them the embarrassment of walking in on Dr. Leland's pre-orientation session.

"What is this? Reality testing?"

"This is where we hold client groups, remember? You haven't facilitated a client group since last year. Since–"

"I know."

"What are you doing here?" she asked.

"What are you doing here?"

"Charlie, it's me. Clare."

"And it's Monday, and what's-his-name is president. I had an English muffin for breakfast."

"You're hopeless," she said.

Attitudinal change frequently corresponds with behavioral change, but it is not a reliable predictor of behavioral change (Liebowitz 1998). Change in attitude can only be measured subjectively and is therefore discounted (Sulk 1999).

"Have you had lunch yet?" he asked.

"It's a bit early, isn't it?"

"Where are you heading?"

"Need to interview a prospective client," she said. "I don't like to be late with borderlines." She looked at her watch and swallowed. "I have five minutes."

"Come sit in my car?"

"No, Charlie." She stepped back and examined his face. "When did you get so creepy?"

He tried to resist looking over his shoulder.

"Let me guess. This is about Barbara?"

"Who said this was *about* anything?"

"Just a feeling." She rolled her eyes and knit her fingers like a schoolgirl called to stand in front of class. "*Okaaay*," she said. "We're making small talk, right? What did you think of that thunderstorm last night?"

"I didn't notice."

"I can't believe that. I couldn't sleep. It felt like my house was going to collapse around me."

"What do you think about professional courtesy?"

"Let it go, Charlie."

"Does she ever…"

"Got to run."

"mention…"

"No!"

"…my name?"

1:15 p.m.

When all were seated, Charlie began. "Glad you could make it, Edelman." Edelman needed special acknowledgment in groups, though it didn't seem to matter what kind. "Hi Burns. Hi Dover. Howdy Dickerson." He put his hands in his pockets. "Sorry for the rescheduling. Miscommunication," he said. "Apparently."

"Shit happens," said Edelman.

The center of Dover's forehead showed one thick crease dividing into three above the bridge of her nose. "I don't see why this meeting was so urgent," she said. "Why did we have to meet at all?"

Dickerson and Burns nodded.

Edelman grinned. "Charlie gets lonely?"

"I mean," Dover said, "these new contracts are the same as the old ones. Is the font bigger?"

"I think the word **notify** is in bold now," said Burns.

Dickerson sighed. "And before you hyphenated *self-harm.* Though in this version–"

"It should be hyphenated," Dover said.

"Good," Charlie said. "That's why meetings like this are so valuable."

Dover: "I had two intakes this morning."

Burns: "I've got Living Skills Assessments to complete."

Edelman: "I was going to wash and wax my old Saab. Why don't you join me, Charlie?"

"Um," Charlie muttered.

"Come on. I have a couple of Heinekens in the fridge."

Since 10/11/04

Of all the ways Charlie thought about Barbara Leland, none were tolerable. She was often a shock to the system: blinking emergency lights, the harsh bleat of an alarm, and momentary paralysis. But he pulled himself through with deep breaths and a simple mantra. *Forward.*

Sometimes, he deliberately conjured an image of her to insulate himself against future shocks. She was coming down the gangway, for example. One in a crowd coming toward him; unnatural light bouncing off her bouncing hair. She wore a magenta scarf, black tights, and sensible suede shoes with gum soles. She was weighed down by her carry-ons but only barely so, because her force, like his against the felt rope and the uniformed airport security... It was as if he and Barbara were in an invisible rip tide; their hearts drowning, reaching.

Or he was in the kitchen making coffee when he felt her at his back. He licked his fingers to separate one paper filter from another. She said, "Let me do that" and placed his fingers in her warm mouth. She guided his hand under her blouse in slow circles around her left nipple.

Forward.

He sprayed the top of his desk with three-tenths ammonia solution. He wiped it with vigor.

2/6/05, 9 a.m.

"Here's the situation," Dr. Donleavy said. "What are you doing?"

"What?"

"The chair. It's clean. Sit."

Charlie sat.

"Think back to our Interdisciplinary Team Meeting a month ago. Do you remember Barbara's budget breakdown?"

She wore a green silk top that day. She wouldn't even look in his direction. He wondered if *breakdown* was a conscious choice.

"Specifically, do you remember her plan to reduce costs?"

"I objected."

"You object to everything." Dr. Donleavy gave Charlie the patented look of concern/ annoyance. "Let me put it this way. Either we cut overhead or cut salaries, and the union won't let us cut salaries. I'll have to cut a position." He licked his thumb.

"I don't envy you, Dr. Donleavy."

"I'm talking about your position, Charlie."

Charlie needed his hand to close his jaw.

"I'm shocked that you're surprised. You didn't see this coming?"

His head shook no, but yes, he had seen it coming. They had been chipping away at his job since Christmas, and yes, he was surprised like a paratrooper whose turn had come to jump. The ground below was burning.

"Is there something you want to say?"

Nothing.

"Look, Charlie. People are talking. The word I'm hearing is 'preoccupied.' I heard it from Clare, Lisa, and some of your residence supervisors. Even Edelman."

"What did he say?"

"You need to get laid."

"And Dr. Leland?"

"She asked her opinion be kept in confidence." Dr. Donleavy pulled a binder from his shelf. On the spine in small print: U/A Log.

"You want me to pee in a cup?"

"No, Charlie."

"I'm not on drugs–"

"Charlie."

"Yesterday I had a beer with Edelman. *Two* beers."

Donleavy opened the binder and pushed it across his desk. "The agency has twelve facilities. We serve roughly three hundred clients at any given time. Of these, eighty percent are subject to drug tests three times per week."

Charlie knew all of what he was being told, but a thought went through his mind like a gunshot. With it came a profound change of disposition. Giddiness. Maybe Donleavy wanted him to collaborate with Dr. Leland on the budget. Maybe she asked for his assistance. Her office perhaps. After hours She was a sly one.

"In front of you," Dr. Donleavy said, "are receipts from the lab." He pointed to the bottom of the page. "The cost to analyze a single urine sample."

"They're squeezing us dry."

"We looked at other labs," he said.

"But this is the going rate."

"Very amusing, Charlie."

"Well, count me in."

"Sit. I'm not finished." The look he gave Charlie was now pure annoyance. "We'll continue to take samples. It's an effective deterrent, and, of course, it's part of our contract with County Mental Health."

"Of course."

"Your job," he said.

"My job?"

"Is to collect the urine that we don't bring to the lab and catalog it. After three weeks, if there are no instructions to the contrary, dispose of it."

"You're joking."

"Not at all."

"And what about my supervisory responsibilities? What about the job I was hired to do?"

"For the time being," he said, "you're relieved of all other duties."

4/21/04

Charlie first met Dr. Barbara Leland in San Francisco at a conference on Separation Anxiety. He needed to fill his annual hours of training, which was a licensing requirement, and the alternatives were Dysthymic Disorder in Cloverdale or STD's in East Oakland. An easy choice. There was a sushi place in San Francisco that he liked, and a pleasant green park only blocks from the hotel.

Dr. Barbara Leland had newly arrived from Boston where she had worked with autistic adolescents; she announced as much in the introductory greetings. Her eyes watered when she said it was hard for her to leave her patients, but she needed a change.

Another trainee, Frank, confided that he had never heard of Separation Anxiety. "I'm here because my agency's footing the bill," he said. "And because if I see another slide show about gonorrhea, I'm going to lose it."

Frank sat between Dr. Leland and Charlie. They each looked at him and one another. Charlie noticed her mild scorn transform ever so slightly into a smile. So, it began: her smile, his sympathetic smile, and his inability to focus on the pretest or the Venn Diagrams on the overhead projector. Even before the morning icebreaker, he was contemplating asking Dr. Leland to lunch.

All were instructed to count off. Frank and four others were twos. Dr. Leland, Charlie, an obese woman named Carmine, a shy Filipina, and a man with a large bandage on his neck were ones. All were asked to describe a memory of a painful separation. The presenters hovered around the room like proctors, and Charlie had been amused as if they thought they might catch him cheating.

Now, he wondered if they weren't making different kinds of observations with another agenda altogether. He has considered that Carmine, the Filipina, the bandaged man, and even Frank were confederates. Nights when he had lost his mantra in the dark, he considered many things. Why would she have said she was dying to try sushi. Surely, she had had plenty of opportunities. Subjective accounts of intense emotional experiences tend to be nonlinear (Kimmelman & Bebe 1983).

Carmine told the group that she had suffered night terrors at age six. She had no idea what brought them on, but she remembered sleeping by her mother's bedroom door because she was afraid her mother might abandon her.

The bandaged man had lost a piece of his larynx to throat cancer. He said he didn't think his anxiety was typical of the disorder that they had come to study, but he remembered looking at himself in the mirror frequently to be sure he hadn't lost any other parts. After he finished, Charlie noticed him nervously touching his ears and the back of his head.

The Filipina, barely audibly, said that she had become homesick at overnight camp. When she returned home, she wanted only to sit in the kitchen. She blubbered that it was "to help Auntie roll lumpia."

Charlie had been an only child and often lonely. But he had no recollection of trauma or profound loss. Nor did he have to his knowledge *then* any irrational fear of loss. From his early years, he remembered a dark cloud had come to visit and that it never really passed. He felt embarrassed to offer nothing, particularly after the woman before him had spoken with such emotion. He simply made something up about a lost puppy.

Charlie didn't often lie; but given the concern in the faces of his peers, he supposed he had given a convincing account.

The bandaged man said, "I hear you, buddy."

Carmine blew her nose in a Kleenex.

Dr. Leland asked the name of his sweet little puppy, and he felt heat rise in his face before he stammered, "Benson."

Dr. Leland described an autistic boy who walked with mincing steps, always a pair of pencils behind his ears. "With his long bangs and his head tilted down, the tips of those pencils poked up like small horns." She laughed, but then her smile dissolved, and her voice grew quiet as if the boy was standing in front of her. "His eyes… Whenever I got to see them, it was a gift."

Charlie studied Dr. Leland's eyes: green and brown, rippling like a reflection of leaves on a pond.

At lunch, over a plate of unagi maki, she put her hand on his. "I don't know why, but I trust you, Charlie."

"I'm glad to hear it. Really."

"I'm learning to trust myself again," she said. "It's not easy, you know."

Charlie's mother had passed away six months earlier, and within a week his father followed her into the grave. His dentist moved to Hawaii, and when Charlie started with a new dentist, the receptionist wanted to know who to contact in case of an emergency. It was routine. Any name and phone number; there *must* be someone. There wasn't. It dawned on him then that he was truly alone in the world. No one had touched him in years.

"Not easy," he said. "I *do* know." But Charlie's mind spun. Where would she live? Where would she work? The cost of an apartment in San Francisco was prohibitive. He could help her find work in the North Bay.

"I can't believe I'm eating eel," she said.

He swallowed, "You can stay with me, Dr. Leland, you know, until -"

"Wow, Charlie."

"You get on your feet."

"Wow."

"Until you get settled."

"Call me Barbara."

"Until you get settled, Barbara."

2/6/05, 11:35a.m.

"We'll save if we reuse the plastic vials."

"Will they need to be sterilized?"

"Easily done."

"Charlie can do it."

"Where?"

"We'll rent a place."

"Won't that cost more?"

"In the short run."

"What will we call this place?"

"Piss Palace." *Laughter.*

"The Super Bowl." *Laughter.*

"The Mental Health Refuse Center."

"Shall we call him in?"

"He's probably standing by the door."

Late Spring to Mid-Fall/04

Charlie wasn't himself, or if so, he was no self he had ever met before. May through August, he was lighthearted, in love. The pleasure of introducing Dr. Leland to sushi was only the first of many. He showed her beaches: river and ocean. Sandy, rocky, and grassy. Museums: the Miwok, the Pomo, paintings and photos of vineyards in every kind of light, and even the Charles Schulz Museum. He had never seen humor in Charlie Brown, but with her, he howled. Together, they did garden tours and jazz, blues, reggae, and Klezmer festivals. Movies in the park. They hurried home from work, exchanged their leather bags for backpacks and a basket. Summer was their sunflower, big as a straw hat. Sweet plums fell into their open palms.

Imagine shy, narrow Charlie was now the ambassador of adventure. He seemed to like nature. He suddenly had a wealth of information on subjects ranging from the healing properties of mineral baths to the fermentation of fortified wines. He would not stop talking unless Dr. Leland pressed her soft lips onto his.

"Oh Charlie," she'd say.

Remember Butch Cassidy driving Etta Place on the handlebars of his bicycle? BJ Thomas strumming, "Raindrops Keep Falling on My Head?" Charlie and Barbara: one long sun-dappled montage.

In September and October, clouds closed in. Perhaps the bike tires were losing air. The soundtrack seemed more like Bergman or Fassbinder. She needed more alone time. Their love making, which had always been so free, became tentative, somber, and much less frequent. Suddenly, they were in real time, and their scripts were indecipherable. She made numerous trips back to Boston, and after each one, she returned less fully.

The honeymoon was over. What they were feeling was expected. At least Barbara seemed to think so, and she found supporting anecdotal evidence from Lisa and Clare. But Charlie wasn't feeling that way. This relationship business was brand new, and the last thing he wanted to hear was what to expect.

One day, she balled a dish towel in her fist and threw it at the back of his head. "Charlie, look at the world!"

"I've been looking," he said. "Never so beautiful!"

"Do we deserve to be happy? How can we?"

"I don't presume to–"

"You have to."

"Why?"

She turned away, plunged her face into her apron. "Nothing lasts forever."

"What we have is something, not nothing. I know nothing about nothing."

She sobbed. "That's...my...point..."

10/21/04

Another return from Boston. Charlie met her at the airport. He had missed her singing in the morning, a sweet melody that filled the house.

They fed each other slices of a California Roll, drank a peppery Chardonnay, and made love. He slept well, better than in a long time.

In the morning, she looked troubled though. "Why Benson?" she asked. "It's a funny name for a puppy, isn't it?" It was Sunday, approaching noon. Thin rapid clouds were visible through a gap in the blinds. They were in his bed. She sat naked on top of the comforter, eating yogurt-covered pretzels from a plastic bag.

He enjoyed touching her bare shoulder and watching the goose bumps rise. "Look," he said. "Now your whole back is covered."

"I'm cold."

"Get in." He patted the space beside him.

"Tell me about Benson."

"What?"

"Your puppy."

"Why drag up sad memories?"

"I've told you everything," she said. "I have."

She had told him how her father cheated and made her mother believe their sadness was all her fault. Her motivation to study psychology was out of a desire to relieve her mother's pain and to protect herself from the same. She had told him about her first period during a gymnastics tournament and a dozen other embarrassing events from high school, including once having tried to end her life with a bottle of erythromycin, the resulting constipation. She told him about her lovers: the concert pianist, the grad school advisor, and the Sri Lankan yoga instructor. She had been deeply in love with each, and the yogi had given her such orgasms, but each of them had let her down.

She couldn't tolerate lies. She said she had wondered if that was why she was drawn to autistics. And she had told him in detail about her autistic teens: pencil boy, ceiling fan girl, the rocker, the math genius, and the girl who knelt on the rug and rested her chin on your knee like a dog. "They hide," she had said, "but they don't lie. They can't."

Charlie went under the covers. She knew him as well as anyone had ever known him. For example, she was the first ever to penetrate him during intercourse. The result was messy and embarrassing, but she was kind. Also, she and Charlie attended agency trainings about motivational interviewing. Together, they learned what resistance looks like. They had even learned about what people do with their eyes when they're fabricating.

"What kind of puppy was he?"

"The little kind."

"Come on, Charlie. I want to know."

"Cute. Fluffy. A mix."

"What happened?"

"I said he ran away."

"How?"

"The way puppies run, diagonally. His tail curled in a cross breeze."

"Where did he go?"

"Through a hole in a fence and into woods."

"What kind of fence was it?"

"What kind of fence?"

"That's what I asked."

"I feel like I'm being interrogated."

"Look at me, Charlie."

He surfaced.

"The fence?"

Before he could answer, a yogurt-covered pretzel bounced off his cheek.

"Barbara," he said.

"Don't call me that. Don't look at me."

He watched as she dressed and packed. He might have said that he never felt so helpless, but that was just the beginning.

2/6/05, 5:15p.m.

Dr. Liebowitz had been one of Charlie's instructors at Sonoma State. He had once said to Charlie, "You have a small mind, perfect for this kind of work. Observe and record. Don't try to interpret."

Once, as they were walking toward coffee, Dr. Liebowitz said, "See that boy? See that girl?" A young man and woman in flip-flops, baggy shorts, and T-shirts, were crossing campus. Their hair was wet as if they'd just come from a shower. They walked side by side on a cedar path, approaching The Quad where other young women and men were sprawled out on the grass. Dr. Liebowitz stopped and covered his eyes.

"Now, she will take his arm," he said. "He will look at her face. He will look at the other faces in the crowd. She will look around too, but she'll really be watching him."

"Yes," Charlie said. "Incredible."

"What does it mean?"

"They're in love?"

"Don't be silly. Are they still locked at the elbows?"

"No. He's bumping knuckles with one of his friends."

"Her hands are deep in her pockets?"

"Yes."

"Shoulders pulled in tight?"

"Yes!"

"My hypothesis," Liebowitz said.

"Go for it."

"If he reaches for her hand in the next fifteen seconds, their relationship will last at least until the end of the semester."

"Amazing," Charlie said. "Absolutely amazing."

He figured that he could use expert help. He had heard that Dr. Liebowitz retired, so he went to see him at his home in Cotati. *He must be seventy-five years old*, Charlie thought.

"He would've been seventy-five," his wife told him on the front stoop, "if he hadn't gassed himself six months ago."

"You're kidding," Charlie said.

"Does that sound like a joke to you?"

"No, I mean–"

"He used the new car. He could've used the old one."

"That's horrible."

"What did you expect? The man thought of human beings as rats, as numbers." She stepped back and let the plexiglass door wheeze behind her.

"I thought of him as a mentor."

"He never mentioned you." She crossed the living room into a dark hall, perhaps headed back to bed. She was in her housecoat. She turned, picked up a wax banana, and dusted it on her sleeve. "What do you want?"

"Understanding," Charlie said.

"He couldn't have helped you."

"He understood people," Charlie pleaded. His anxiety piqued, terror rising. He was experiencing nine of the thirteen symptoms of a panic attack (DSM-IV).

She approached him slowly and unevenly – a bad hip. She put her hands on his arms. Her swollen thumbs in the pits of his elbows. Her eyes had once been pretty. "Dr. Liebowitz understood how to predict observable behavior under very controlled circumstances. He knew nothing about hearts." She opened her purse and took out a card. "Here. Call this man. Tell him Edie sent you."

11/14/04

Weeks passed, and Barbara Leland hadn't called. Charlie didn't know her number. She wasn't at work. Finally, Charlie spoke to Jennie in payroll and learned that Dr. Leland cashed in her vacation, sick, and float days and borrowed on what hadn't yet accrued.

"How much did she borrow?" Charlie asked.

"Um. None of your business?"

"Please Jennie."

"I've told you too much already." She bit her pen and squinted. "I don't like that look in your eyes."

"I'm worried about her."

"Stalker."

Hours later, his exhaustion caught up with him. He collapsed and drifted out to sea on a mattress. It was drenched and slowly sinking. He could see his parents on shore. He hollered. "Mom! Dad!" But they were busy folding their beach towels. Then he was making love to Barbara. He was on top, thrusting. He cried out, "Where did you go?" Or something unintelligible but that seemed to be the intent. When Charlie woke, he thought, *I'm a helpless child.*

He changed his boxers and pulled on a shirt, and trousers.

He drove to the office and waited for the night janitor to take his smoke break. He slipped through an unlocked door and rifled through Jennie's files until he found what he needed. Given the hours accrued and hours spent, Dr. Leland absolutely had to be back in time for the Christmas party.

2/7/05

He lived in a modest cabin several hundred feet from the Russian River. When Charlie greeted him, he was hosing mud off the base of a shed in his backyard. He was shirtless, tall and lean with a slight curve in his upper back. A gray ponytail. He must have been in his mid-seventies, and he was not what

Charlie expected at all. He should've been dead; he had a building named after him!

"Thanks for seeing me, Dr. Sulk."

He smiled. "Edie thought I might be able to help. Who knows?" He dropped the hose and lead Charlie back to his house with one big hand on Charlie's shoulder. Years ago, in school, Charlie had read his *Statistical Analysis of Human Change,* which was required for a class with Dr. Liebowitz. Of his own initiative, Charlie read the classic *The Meaning of Charting.* He was a giant in the field.

Two golden retrievers bounded toward them. The dogs quickly examined Charlie's crotch and then dove upon Dr. Sulk's knees until he squatted to scratch their heads. He seemed almost as excited as they were. Was this some special reunion? "Happens twenty times a day," he explained. "They forget me when I'm out of sight." Walking again, he put his hand on Charlie's shoulder. "They remind me of now," he said. "I don't know what I'd do without them."

They sat in a cool dark room lined with bookshelves. He poured two glasses of iced tea. "Tell me, Charlie. Who you are and what ails you?"

Charlie described a feedback loop of pain and humiliation. Though he didn't know how it started, he saw it more clearly than he ever had. Dr. Sulk listened, interrupting only briefly for clarification.

They heard a car door shut. Then another. Sulk's five-year-old grandson entered with no less enthusiasm than the golden retrievers. The doctor offered him the kind of careful attention he had given to Charlie as the boy described every scene from Shrek III. Charlie wondered if the man was capable of averting his attention or if he might not have some mild, pleasant form of dementia.

"Dr. Sulk," Charlie said. "I have to confess. I thought you were deceased. Sulk Mental Health Center?"

He laughed hard. "My brother, Dr. Sulk, was a behavioral scientist and died ten years ago."

"Oh?"

"What a mean little man he was."

"Really?"

He looked at Charlie with his persistent eager smile.

"I assumed that the wife of Dr. Liebowitz, and well, the name Dr. Sulk. I mean–"

"I treated Edie's bunny," he said. "It had been hit by a car. I'm a veterinarian." Again, he laughed. "What a charming woman. How is she?"

"I don't know. But I didn't come here to talk about her."

"Of course," he said. "You were telling me about Benson. Please go on."

"You've missed the point. There was no Benson. I invented Benson."

"Out of nothing?" he said. "That seems doubtful." He refilled Charlie's tea. "Relax. It will come to you."

12/22/04

For the last nine years in a row, the Christmas Party had been held at The Hyatt in Santa Rosa. It was a plush in a cost-effective way. The administrators, the clinicians, and the folks from payroll seemed all pleasantly surprised by the quantity of shrimp or the graciousness of service. But more importantly, they seemed thankfully unsurprised. They knew what to expect. As an agency, they were temperate in their habits.

When they drank, danced, flirted, or expressed their politics, they did so with a burdensome awareness that they were models of mental health. They arrived at parties in slightly more than workaday colorful attire. Their shirts were opened one button lower than usual. The crowd was filled with vinyl and leather jackets, holding the shape of the hanger that had held them every other day of the year. They congregated in small groups with cocktails in hand. They fussed over the dip. They laughed too long and loud about the most mundane nonsense . Or could it have been that Charlie was in an altered mood?

He had wanted the courage to tell the truth. Fuck the eggnog because beside the punchbowl was a half-gallon of Captain Morgan's Spiced Rum. As the evening wore on, he felt that he had obligations: to inform Jennie that some men had good intentions, to enable Lisa to chuckle at her own self-importance, to make Dr. Donleavy aware of his nervous tic. In a hushed tone, he told one of the pretty servers – the one with a nose ring and micro-braids – that though no one else seemed to notice, he knew she was whoring herself working for Hyatt. When he saw Edelman, he felt a compulsion to give him a high five. He pushed through three clusters of cocktail sippers before he stumbled into Dr. Leland.

"Hi Charlie," she said and embraced him. To his surprise, she went right back into her conversation, a comparison of real estate values on east and west coasts. It was as if nothing had ever happened between them.

"Welcome back, Dr. Leland," he said.

"Please, call me Barbara." She laughed and sipped her drink. She turned back to who she was talking to. "When you factor in the higher cost of heating, you're really paying about the same for a one bedroom."

"But you told me not to call you that." He took her drink out of her hand and drank it. "Those were the last words you said to me. Remember?"

"Not here, Charlie. Please."

"Don't you remember?" He shouted. "Don't you remember telling me you loved me? Don't you remember shoving your finger in my asshole?"

Exactly what followed wasn't clear. Charlie now knew what it cost to replace a punchbowl at The Hyatt. He shouted more, but he had no memory of what he said. Dr. Leland's friends closed in around her like muscles around a slipped disc and escorted her away.

Charlie only knew what Edelman told him days after the event. "You jumped onto a table," he said. "Must've been three feet. You quoted a guy named Liebowitz. Something about the effective use of negative re-enforcers. You wanted us, individually and collectively, to know we were engaged in a sham. 'We don't know what makes people change,' you said. 'We don't have a fucking clue.'"

3/8/05

Charlie visited Dr. Sulk three times in the next three weeks. They wandered the dimly lit halls of Charlie's childhood in search of Benson. His family never had any pets, because his father was allergic to fur.

"How sad," Dr. Sulk said.

Charlie told him that he'd had a little brother – named Jackson – who died just ten days after he was born.

"Also sad," Sulk said, "but interesting. Benson. Jackson. Memory is often imprecise." Dr. Sulk promised that they were getting closer to understanding. But Charlie was doubtful. He wasn't sure that he wanted to rediscover Benson. What could it possibly mean? Still, he enjoyed the company of Dr. Sulk and found that he could carry Sulk's gentle, inquisitive nature into his own daily routines.

Friday afternoons had almost always been hard for Charlie. Coworkers made plans for the evening, excitement in the air. At such times, his loneliness was palpable. He preferred to be away from the office at the end of the week.

For his new assignment, he had one small room with a large basin and another smaller room with a single desk. No one ever dropped by. No one called. Was it a curse or a blessing?

The phone rang for the first time ever, and Charlie let it. One. Two. Three. With a lukewarm vial of urine in his hand, he picked it up. "MHRC."

"What?"

"MHRC."

"What?"

"Mental Health Refuse Center."

"It's Lisa. Can you come down to the office?"

"I suppose what I'm doing can wait."

"Come right away," she said. "Barbara wants to talk."

Involuntarily, he released the vial. It fell upon the edge of the desk and splashed onto his trousers. After brushing vigorously with a moist towel, he hopped into his car and headed downtown.

Why did people change? Charlie didn't have a fucking clue.

There was a yellow light at the intersection of Fourth and Mendocino. He could have accelerated and passed under it as the young man in the monster truck behind him would have wanted. But he didn't. He chose to wait. In that moment, he chose to remember what had escaped him for so many years.

"Please, have a seat," Dr. Donleavy said.

"Barbara asked for this meeting," Lisa said.

"Because I'm leaving," Dr. Leland said.

"Oh."

"I didn't wipe your name off the dry-erase board," she said.

"Okay."

"You loved me?"

Charlie nodded, but what he felt was detached, mildly curious, and bored. He felt as if some great tension had been released, discharged. But why? *A horn blared. The ripe smell of piss.* "I think so."

"Because if that's what you call love, Charlie, then Jesus. I'd hate to see–"

"Let's try to keep our focus," Dr. Donleavy interrupted.

She took a breath and started again. "My father is dying, Charlie. I saw him. When I went back to Boston, I saw… Oh, it has been twenty years… I didn't ever expect... I told myself I never would, but–"

"I get it," Charlie said.

"Get what?"

"You're ready to move on. I am too."

"You can't get it. I haven't said it."

"Of course, but–"

"You see," Dr. Leland swallowed, looking at Lisa. Lisa pointed at Charlie. Dr. Leland looked at Charlie. "You see, I thought I loved you, but I only loved the idea of you." Her mouth quivered; she wept.

Charlie thought he should weep. A better Charlie would have wept, but nothing came. He would have handed her a Kleenex, but Lisa beat him to the box.

"When I saw my father, helpless, and intubated, it was as if all my ideas and feelings changed," Dr. Leland said.

"What they call reforming a primary cathexis."

"Well, yes. But nothing is so simple."

"Nothing *is* simple. Or simpler. That is what I have come to too. Also."

A long silence followed. Dr. Donleavy cleared his throat and told Charlie that he could have his former position back on a trial basis. Charlie declined. He tried to assure Dr. Donleavy and Lisa that he was happy at the MHRC – it was where he belonged now. They gave him the patented look. Lisa opened a window.

Charlie apologized for the foul smell. "I had an accident," he said. To clear up any confusion, he added, "It wasn't my urine."

Dr. Leland stood. Charlie stood. But Dr. Donleavy and Lisa remained in their seats, presumably to process what had just occurred. So, after those long months apart, he was at last alone with her in the parking lot. Or almost alone because Clare was waiting in the driver's seat of her car.

Dr. Leland's suitcase was visible through the rear window. She told Charlie that she had been staying with Clare until it was time to fly back east. "I'm sorry, Charlie. I never meant to hurt you."

He breathed in deep and breathed out – a practice he had developed with Dr. Sulk. He could see her as he had never seen her, a complete and separate being. He had rehearsed a thousand speeches for a moment just like this, but he felt no obligation to speak. He felt a fleeting urge to share his new revelation, the true origin of Benson. But he breathed, and the urge passed.

"Goodbye, Charlie."

"Goodbye, Dr. Leland."

She walked toward Clare's car, the *clop-clop* of her heels on the pavement. Her hair bounced gently. Her arm that swings swung by her side. Then it stopped. She stopped. She turned around and came back toward Charlie. She stood in front of him, one foot away, and reached for his hand.

3/9/05

"And then what happened?"

"I told you, Dr. Sulk. She put her card in my hand. She said to call her. She said I could drive her to the airport if I wanted to. She said that she wanted me to."

"Of course. Have you called her?"

"No. I wanted to talk to you first."

"It's the phone. Hold on."

"I was a bed wetter," Charlie blurted. "Dr. Sulk, Benson was..."

Sulk nodded. He excused himself into the kitchen.

Charlie followed into the doorway and listened.

"It's time to let go," Dr. Sulk said. "The Russian Dwarf only lives about three years. The cost of removing a tumor...the risk. I just don't think it's worth it. You'll think of something to tell her."

"Okay," Sulk continued, offering Charlie a smile. The telephone was still pressed to his ear. "Do you have a tree in your backyard, Chrissie? Is it cool underneath? When the time comes, your mother will help you find a shovel and a small, pretty box."

Dr. Sulk returned to sit beside Charlie. "I'm retired," he explained, "but former clients still call." He opened his eyes. "I'm ready."

"Benson Inc. was printed on the dial of my moisture alarm!"

Dr. Sulk smiled and waited.

"My mother used to lie in bed with me until I'd fall asleep. But when Jackson was born, she stopped. Soon after, I started wetting the bed. The alarm was something my mother rigged up to help me. She'd kiss me, and she'd say, 'Good night, Charlie. Good night, Benson.'"

"Secondary enuresis," Dr. Sulk said. "And I suppose the alarm frightened you?"

"At first it did. But later, no. Not at all. Benson became my best friend. After Jackson died, it became so smothering in that house, day after day. Hushed tones. Sour expressions." Charlie rested his head on his hand. "Sometimes it seemed as if my mother and father were afraid to look at one another or me." His eyes teared. "I think they were afraid to acknowledge the limits of their love – like they had spent it. Like they had no more to give one another or me."

"Sad." Dr. Sulk wagged his head. "And you continued to wet the bed?"

"I was a torrent."

"And your mother and father were angry about it?"

"They were furious. They took Benson away."

"They took Benson away?" He looked puzzled, then gave his head a shake. "Life is a succession of losses and paltry replacements. The sooner we accept that, the happier we can be."

"I guess so," Charlie said. "Wow, do you really believe that?"

"Sounds a little heavy, doesn't it?

"What do you believe, Dr. Sulk?"

"Mature love is as rare as a three-legged lop-ear."

"And you've seen a three-legged lop-ear?"

"A number of times, yes. Tell me more about your farewell to Barbara Leland."

"I can't."

"Oh?"

"She, um."

"Breathe Charlie." Dr. Sulk leaned forward in his chair, rested one of his big hands on Charlie's shoulder. "Why don't you finish about the moisture alarm? That's what you wanted to talk about."

Charlie sat up straighter and the color returned to his cheeks. "Belt it out, Benson, I used to say. Mom and Dad want you to keep quiet, but I want to hear you. I need to hear your voice."

"Ah," Dr. Sulk raised his glass, "One more shrill song."

"For love!" Charlie said.

"For love?" Dr. Sulk said.

"Yes."

"For love?" Dr. Sulk laughed. "You're kidding! What you're describing is an aberration, but–"

"I wish you wouldn't say that."

"Charlie."

"I still love Benson."

"*Charlie.*"

"What?"

"I'm going to bring you a change of pants."

"Oh. I'm so sorry. I–"

"And then I'm going to bring you the phone."

"What?"

"Call her."

"What?"

"Call Barbara. I'll sit right here by your side."

Down the Ocean

It's a sticky June night in 1977, the year, btw, a miniseries called *Roots* blew up the last of our black and white televisions, the year Elvis wiggled into the next life, the year a film called Star Wars stimulated our imaginations like nothing before and perhaps nothing after. Mick, btw, was on the cusp of puberty, leaning down a hill toward a cold bottle of Yoo-hoo when he heard a *hey* from the corner with a blinking streetlight.

"Hey Mick! What's up, man?"

"Nothing much."

"Been wanting to talk with you." Donald Hagner pulls two Marlboros from the breast pocket of his black vinyl jacket. "Smoke?"

"I guess." Mick has never even put his lips on a butt before. The first puff isn't bad, but the second he draws deep into his lungs and coughs so hard that he has to sit on the curb to catch his breath.

"Things are pretty harsh, man," Donald says. "Gotta quit, myself." He takes a long, deep drag. "That's what I want to talk about: quitting." His manner seems so practiced and strange that Mick feels he has stumbled into an episode of *Starsky & Hutch*. "My lawns love me," Donald says, "'cause I always do a kick-ass job."

"Your lawns?" Mick asks.

"Shit, yeah. West Park, Poplar, and Birch, except for what's taken by the brothers down Gwynn Oak, all the lawns 'round here are mine."

"That's cool," Mick says, but he thinks Donald is the jerk he has always thought he was. Now, he wants to brag about his lawns.

"I'm only telling you this 'cause I want out. Got something much sweeter, you know." He blows a smoke ring through a smoke ring. "I want to make sure my lawns are taken care of in case I decide to come back to them."

"You want to give me your lawns?"

"You can even use my machine. Front-wheel drive."

"That's cool!"

"But I'm a businessman."

"You want a cut of the money?"

"Nah. That's chicken shit." Donald spits. "Don't get me wrong. Cutting grass is an excellent way to get started." He steps on his cigarette. "You headed down the hill? Come on."

Mick destroyed his lawnmower earlier in the day when he pushed it under a holly bush, and it bit into the cap of a sewer pipe. What an ugly sound: coughing oil and smoke. He wanted to run away. It was the second time in a week he'd damaged the thing.

"Typical carelessness," he heard his mother say. He got silence from his father who was oblivious to lawn care and who had with some apparent reluctance retreated in the battle to develop the boy's character. Mick's mother said that Mick would have to pay for repairs this time, and Moe, the small engine repairman, said that he'd be better off buying a new one. It would take seven weeks of Mick's earnings to buy the cheapest machine at Sears. He wanted to run, simply run away. Who would've thought archrival grass cutter, Donald Hagner, would rescue the summer?

Donald is sixteen, three years older than Mick, and a junior at Woodlawn Senior. He'd been in the lawn care business four years, and he'd be the first to say it's boring, but he'll also tell you it's how he got where he is. He had never been popular in the neighborhood. He doesn't play football or baseball and doesn't have a skateboard. He prefers disco to rock 'n' roll, and he'd been tagged with the nickname, Hagmanure. But one rarely hears Hagmanure anymore since he started cutting and selling grass. Some of the kids on the block now wear the same silk shirts and designer jeans that Donald seems to have always worn.

Donald's parents, like Mick's parents, make their livings outside Woodlawn. Like the Connellys, the Hagners are private people, but that's as far as the likeness goes. The Connellys are ten years older than Mr. Hagner, and twenty years older than his wife. Mr. and Mrs. Connelly are professionals and work downtown in Baltimore. Most of the adults in Woodlawn push paper at the Social Security Administration. Others sell clothes, novelties, and flavored popcorn at Security Square Mall. According to Donald, Mr. Hagner works on a military base in Virginia, but he doesn't wear a uniform. Mr. Hagner is a big man with a dark, brooding face. He never talks.

Mrs. Hagner doesn't have a job. She has long, straight black hair and a nose like Cher. Once Mick saw her naked, sunning in her backyard. He had been walking, kicking an empty milk carton against the curb. When he peered over the hedge, she saw him. She didn't scramble to cover herself. She slowly draped a towel over her crotch and thighs. The sight of her bush and her big, brown nipples left Mick burning from his eyes to his swollen shorts.

They walk, but Mick never reaches his bottle of Yoo-hoo. They stop in a patch of woods on the hillside above Gwynn Oak Avenue. Donald opens a plastic bag and packs a wooden pipe with a few pinches of weed. "Mexican," he says.

Mick nods. *Is he referring to the contents or the pipe?*

"This shit'll blow your mind."

They smoke one bowl and then another. When Donald isn't inhaling smoke, he's talking with smoke leaking from his lips. Talking looks difficult, and Mick believes what Donald is saying must be important, but he can't quite take in the words. He's preoccupied with two thoughts: *I'm getting high*, and *this is what high is.*

Other thoughts dogpaddle through his consciousness. *I wonder if Donald knows I saw his mother naked*, and *has he ever seen her naked?* And *am I going to be wearing those silky shirts soon?* And *where did I get my opinion about those shirts anyways?* This last thought is as frightening and strangely sexy as the dull look in Mrs. Hagner's eyes when she saw Mick seeing her. It was not as if she were a mother seeing a boy but like a woman seeing a man. Mick had felt it then as he does now, that his skin doesn't fit.

"Well?" Donald asks. "What's the word, dude?"

If Mick has learned anything in school, it's how to pretend he's been paying attention. Donald's words passed like the bats under the streetlight, and though Mick couldn't follow them in flight, he expects they will circle by again. "Yeah," he says after a long pause, "Ocean City is cool."

"Then you want to do it?"

"But how're we going to get there?"

"You're high, man. But that's cool. It's killer shit." Donald laughs. "I'll find us a ride."

"Cool. When?"

"You're baked!"

Mick laughs. "I guess I am."

"Leave the details to me," Donald says. "Come on. I gotta get my ass home."

Two days pass. Mick puts his hands in his front pockets, his back pockets, and his front pockets again. He knocks on the Hagner's front door. Mr. Hagner appears barely visible behind the sunlit screen.

"I came to borrow Donald's lawnmower," Mick says.

Mr. Hagner opens the door and waits for Mick to step inside.

In a dark corner, Mrs. Hagner sits on the sofa, dressed in black jeans and a bra. The rims of her eyes are pink as if she's been crying. She forces a smile. "Donald's not here," she says. "I'll unlock the garage for you."

Mick follows her through the dining room and into the kitchen. The carpet feels plush, smells new. The furniture has a dark finish and are a matching set, which is so unlike the chairs, tables, and lamps acquired in Mick's house over many years. Each piece with its own dusty history.

The hall is lit by a single red bulb. She leads Mick into the backyard. He looks at the lounge chair upon which he had seen her before. "This way," she says and opens a door into the dark garage. Her voice is matter of fact. "You can wheel it out this way. Don't scratch the car. Mr. Hagner loves his car." She waits in the doorway. A sliver of sunlight on her shoulder and the side of her face. "Is Donald your friend?"

"Yeah," Mick says. "I guess so. He's doing me a favor."

"Maybe you're doing him a favor," she says.

"I guess." Mick is puzzled. She seems to be adjusting a clasp in the center of her bra, and he feels an ache in his crotch. He pushes the mower out onto the lawn and swallows hard. "Thank you," he manages.

"I'm glad Donald has a friend." Her smile doesn't seem forced.

"We're going down the ocean," he says. He's nervous. He wants to be friendly.

"You and your family?" she asks.

"Me and Donald."

Her smile turns, a hint of worry. "I didn't know."

Mr. Hagner calls out, "Doris" from the back door, and her face changes. She waves goodbye, an oddly girlish flutter of the hand.

Ocean City is three hours away. People Mick knows don't go for the afternoon; they spend the night or the weekend. His parents worry, sure, but they're not the overprotective types, not always watching like Barry Eberhaus's mom or Terry Noonan's dad. Because of their busy careers and what Mrs. Connelly calls 'Mick's private nature,' they don't pry into his business, and he rarely asks for their involvement. It has been thirty years since they were in their early teens, and it was "a very different world then," as Mrs. Connelly often says. She has told Mick she's troubled by his aloofness, but she believes it will pass like other difficult stages.

Once he overheard her on the telephone talking with a coworker who has a daughter about his age. "His grades in school are mediocre, reportedly a concentration problem. But I've never doubted his intelligence. After all, I'm intelligent." She laughed. "His father is very intelligent. At least he has friends in the neighborhood. That's a good sign. And he's working now."

Sometimes, Mrs. Connelly and Mick work together in the yard. She tries to draw him out and seems amused to hear his strong opinions about how to retain the slope or where to plant the boxwoods. She teases him with her chin resting on the handle of her shovel, "Since when did you become so knowledgeable?" She folds her gloves. "You wouldn't ask your old mother or father about sex. What could *we* possibly know?"

Days later, walking the halls at Our Lady of Perpetual Help, Mick can appreciate the friendly overture, but in the moment, it never fails to give him a shudder. No, he couldn't describe his feelings about girls or sex to his mother or father. No way. And he doesn't want to hear about their experiences. When Mrs. Connelly has shared memories about "how I sat behind your father in graduate school and couldn't see past his large shoulders" or about "what a gentleman your father was" about the time "he drove all the way to Atlantic City to buy me a box of saltwater taffies," Mick could only think, *God, that's another world.* And once he even said so. "Jeez, Mom. God. That's another world."

She looked as if she had swallowed a gnat or as if it had only then occurred to her what a long time ago it was.

What Mick would like to say is, "Mom, Dad, I'm going to Ocean City with my friend, Donald Hagner. I'll be back tomorrow." But that won't fly, and he knows it. If he instead puts it as a question; they tend to come back with many more questions that he can't answer in this case. The times he has asked permission, they've gotten excited like *this* is what it means to be parents. Like they had better have advice and a handful of conditions. He doesn't want that. A plan comes to him at dinner.

"Would you pass the rice pilaf down to your father?" Mrs. Connelly asks.

"I love rice pilaf," Mick says.

"I'm glad to hear it." She looks at her husband, spooning from the big bowl.

"I've been thinking about camping." Mick says. "Barry has an extra sleeping bag -"

"You have your own bag," she says, "and you haven't even used it yet."

"I guess I haven't."

"Let's hear more," Mr. Connelly says.

"Well, Donald Hagner has this cool lantern."

"I didn't know you were friends with Donald Hagner," Mrs. Connelly says.

"He lent me his lawnmower."

"You'd better take care of it," she says.

"We were thinking about camping out. Probably in the Hagners' backyard."

"Oh?" Mrs. Connelly asks.

"When?" Mr. Connelly asks.

"Tomorrow night."

"I guess that'd be okay." Mrs. Connelly looks again at her husband. He puckers his lips and shrugs.

"Watch out for grizzlies," he says.

"And I guess I'll miss dinner, because we're going to cook hot dogs and stuff."

"Is this ground chuck?" Mr. Connelly asks. "It seems pretty lean."

And that's that. After dinner while Mick is rinsing his plate, his mother says, "You know, Mick, I hope I wasn't too hard on you about the broken mower. I'm sure it was an accident. I'm glad to see you've found a way to work it out."

"It's okay, Mom."

She tucks him under the chin and says, "I want to trust you, kiddo."

In the morning, Mick meets Donald at the corner. His light blue bathing suit puffing out from the waist of his jeans, a bedroll under his arm.

"What's that for?"

"I was hoping I could stick it at your house."

"Cool. I'll put it in the garage."

"So, what? Your Mom is going to drive us down the ocean?"

"You're still high." Donald laughs. "Hell man. We got to get our own ride." He stashes the sleeping bag and tip toes around the house. They walk along Gwynn Oak Avenue, and Mick notices Donald frequently looking back over his shoulder. At first, Mick thinks Donald is being overly cautious, afraid that maybe his parents will drive by. Then he remembers that Terry Noonan said, "Hagner got his ass beat by the brothers up Woodlawn High." Mick wants to ask what happened but decides he'll wait until the right time.

Soon, they reach Security Boulevard, several hundred yards from the beltway ramp. Donald opens a small backpack. "Smoke a bowl?"

It doesn't take Mick long to say, "Sure." Five, ten seconds – not a meaningful pause for two boys walking fast down the street, cars and trucks passing; but Mick is thinking as hard as he ever has. His parents would flip out if they knew what he is doing. He's more than a little scared. Going down the ocean is way worse than cutting school or lifting Snickers bars at Woodlawn Drugs. It's even worse than looking at pictures in Hustler, though the feeling is similar in some ways.

Donald leads him to a spot out of sight where the sewer conduit empties into Woodlawn Creek. The air is thick with honeysuckle and skunk cabbage. They smoke two bowls.

Donald says, "I'll cut you in for ten percent this time."

"Ten percent of what?"

"We're gonna get rich, dude. Everybody buys weed down O.C. They'll pay top dollar. I can sell a dime bag for twice what I get here, no problem." Donald stuffs his gear into his backpack, and they start again toward the ramp. "I figure ten percent since I lent you my machine, and shit, I gave you the best lawns in Woodlawn. But in the future, you know, if it goes well, I'll make it a bigger cut." Donald walks ahead with his thumb high in the air. "At first we'll work together. There's an excellent spot outside The Lackawana Club. I'm talking a shit load of green, baby!" He turns to Mick and makes two open fists as if his hands were clamped around two thick stacks of bills. His eyes are big and hungry.

"Wait," Mick says. "Aren't we gonna like swim?"

Donald's eyes remain wide, but his jaw now hangs open, incredulous. It's the first time all morning that the boys have looked each other full in the face. Smoking pot affects Mick's sense of time and vision, and though he hasn't got the words to describe it, he's reminded of comic books. One frame following another with unpredictable gaps in between. Some shots are wide, some close-up. It seems as if someone else is turning the pages. He wants to slow it all down, to study the picture and make the right decision, but behind Donald, he sees a brown and white Ford pickup pull onto the shoulder.

"Holy shit," Donald hollers. "You must be good luck, man." Donald speaks to the strands of bleached blond hair blowing out of the passenger side window. "We're going down the ocean."

"Climb in back," she says. "That's where we're going."

Soon, it's too noisy to carry a conversation. It's the hottest day of the summer so far, but the wind is numbing at seventy-five miles an hour. In three hours, Mick is shivered to exhaustion, and the sun has burned his eyelids. His hair is so full of knots that he can't push his fingers through it.

"Here we are!" Donald leaps from the truck bed. He tries to sell a dime bag to the woman in the front seat. "Panama Red," he tells her.

She lifts her hair off her shoulder and examines it. "Panama Red?" She laughs. "No thanks."

Donald and Mick tear down the frontage road to the main strip. Mick smells the mix of sea air and burning fat. Like always, it gets his heart pounding. He wants a large order of French fries from Thrasher's, two orders. He wants to body surf. He wants to check out the arcade, see what he can win at skee-ball.

Donald, almost breathless, describes the leather jacket he's going to buy with the money they make. He says there's a dance club that Mick would dig, because the foxes are bitchin'. He grabs Mick's forearm, and he lowers his voice as they approach The Lackawana, a bar and package store on the end of the strip.

Meanwhile, back in Woodlawn, Mick's friend, Barry Eberhaus knocks on the Connelly's door. He spins a football on his fingertip. Terry Noonan is standing by the curb. "Is Mick around?" Barry asks.

"I thought he was with you," Mrs. Connelly says. "I thought you boys were camping with Donald Hagner."

"No," says Barry. "No way."

"Well, that's odd," she says.

Barry leaps off the porch and gives the news to Terry.

Mrs. Connelly hears Terry scream, "Camping out with Hagmanure!" When she returns to the kitchen, she describes what she has heard to her husband.

"Watch me," Donald says. He points to a place for Mick to stand against the wood-shingled back side of the building, in the slanted shadows. Donald approaches a man coming from the store. The man has a paper bag in his hand, probably a six pack. "Get high?" Donald asks.

Before he answers, two more men push through the door.

"What ya got?" says the man. He grins at the other two men.

Donald puts his fingers to his lips and inhales.

"But that's illegal," the man says. His friends laugh. Two of the men get into a Buick while the other circles back and says to his friends, "I'll catch up with you." Donald leads him to the side of the building and back into the shadows. The man opens a nickel bag, sniffs, and picks at the buds. "What's this?" he asks.

"Hawaiian."

"Bullshit."

"It's good shit," Donald says.

The man shakes his head. He gets in his van and drives off.

"Now, you get the idea," Donald says to Mick.

"This doesn't seem so cool," Mick replies.

"Oh, it's cool, man. Don't get all chicken shit on me now."

"Hey," Mick says. "I guess I heard something about you getting beat up by black dudes down Gwynn Oak." He watches Donald. If his intention is to slow the action, and he thinks that's what he intended, he gets the desired response. But he gets something else as well.

The swagger is gone. Donald is the Donald of years ago, drawing chalk figures in his family's driveway while Mick and his friends toss a football in the street. They are just two boys far from home, and Mick experiences a shot of fear.

It's a relief when Donald finally speaks. "I don't know who told you that shit," he says. "I never had any trouble with the brothers."

"I guess I just heard it," Mick says.

"You take the next one," Donald says. "Here she comes."

The next one bends her head toward Mick, a concerned face, as if perhaps he is asking directions to the highway. But then she dismisses him with a wave of the hand.

Another is wearing a halter top, and she's sunburnt on the top of her breasts. She says, "Whyn't you boys go have some fun."

The next one says, "I'm the owner of the Lackawana Club." Behind him is a college-age boy in a white apron and with a baseball bat.

Mick and Donald dash under the pylons; shadows racing under their feet. After two blocks, Donald stops and presses his fist into his side. Mick slows briefly, but he can't stop. He waves as if to say, *Come on*, and then, *Goodbye*. He knows he's far from the boy with the bat, but he hoists himself over a fence and runs on the cool, shaded sand until it opens into the wide beach. He finds his stride, running toward the breaking water. Perspiration breaks on his forehead. Running and running between towels and umbrellas, leaping over buckets and shovels and children. Running until he's breathless. He peels off his shoes, pants, and shirt, down to his light blue trunks. He runs, knees chest high into the ocean.

After riding five waves, he can feel his hair matted on his head, burns tightening the skin on his face, and he tastes the salt with his eyes. This might've been fun, he thinks, if Barry and Terry were here. Or even his parents, who are so old and *sensible*. They'd spread out on the beach with their thick novels, deli sandwiches, and thermos of iced tea. If his parents were here, they'd go to Phillip's: crab cakes, a basket of bread, and the starchy white napkin. His mother's embarrassed smile while reminding him to wear the napkin on his lap. All of it…

All of it comes back to him like a flash flood of sadness, loneliness, and guilt; emotions so wide and deep that he can't name them. He has never felt so far from home. A wave catches him from behind and drags him under, whirling, tugging until he is slammed face first into the sandy floor. When he finds his feet, he coughs, and the back of his throat feels as if it has been stung by a bee.

He has lost Donald, and that's okay. Maybe it's for the best. But he's hungry now, and it's getting cold. In his pants, he has ten dollars, but where the hell are his pants? He scans the beach. He walks on the firm sand and tries to orient himself between a blue umbrella and a rainbow-colored towel where he thought he had dropped his clothes. He can only find one of his shoes, and there's a foamy puddle in it.

At quarter to seven, he has one more hour of sunlight. He wanders the beach and the strip and returns to the beach. His skin, shrunken from the burn, shrinks more now in the cold. His lips look blue in an arcade mirror. The sky bleeds into twilight. There seems to be only one choice. He walks the long, flat, two-lane road back to the highway. He should've snatched a towel from the beach to keep warm, but he assures himself that it only takes one ride if you're lucky, and he must be lucky, because the alternatives are too terrible.

He imagines the perfect ride: Mrs. Hagner in her bra. Mrs. Hagner not in her bra. Her brown nipples pointing the way home. He doesn't need to ponder on this long before he has an embarrassing lump in his shorts, and no one's going to pick up a boy with an erection. Or maybe someone would, and that could be worse. He forces himself to imagine other perfect rides. Bruce Springsteen in a souped-up Charger with a double order of fries. He sings as he walks and surprises himself, because he knows all the words to "Born to Run" and most of "Thunder Road."

Few people would be leaving Ocean City at sunset. It's the beginning of the weekend. What little traffic there is is going the other way. But he can't think about that. His singing gets louder, more dramatic and convincing, as the sky darkens. Walking fast, shivering, running, singing, and dreaming up the perfect ride; he almost leaves his fear behind.

An hour and three miles later, a van pulls over to the side. How could the driver have seen Mick in the dark? Mick sprints down the shoulder of the road until he catches hold of the dented chrome latch. He opens the door. It squeals. The driver's hands are large and look orange in the light from the dash. He's a black man. There are half a dozen black kids at Mick's school, but they keep their own company. That's how it has always been. Mick has never gotten into a car with a black man before. He thinks he may have never seen a black person at Ocean City.

"Hey, you're pretty young," the man says. "You must be freezing your ass off." The man clears papers and clothing from the passenger seat while Mick stands with one bare foot on the runner and the other on gravel. *Why*, Mick thinks, *would a black man pick me up*? If Barry were here, he'd say, "You must be fucking crazy to get in a car with a nigger." Mick's parents would say, "We don't use that kind of language," but they would also say, "You haven't shown good judgment today, Mick."

"Name's Rudy," says the black man. "Are you getting in?" Because *this* is the choice that has been presented and because he couldn't say no now, for reasons he can't possibly explain to himself or anyone else, he climbs in.

They shake hands. "I was in the service, and now I'm back," Rudy says. "Just looking to have a little fun before I have to earn a living." His smile is huge. "A living? *This* is living!" He says he'd done plenty of hitching in his life, and he knows what that's all about. "You must be hungry." He has a sixteen-ounce bag of crab-flavored potato chips between the seats. He hands the bag over to Mick. "There's half a strawberry milkshake if you want it. I can't finish it."

It has been a day of surprises, but what surprises Mick most of all is that Rudy, a complete stranger, seems to regard him like another adult. "Do you drive?" Rudy asks. "Don't worry about it. I'm just glad to have some company, because the highway gets pretty fucking boring sometimes." Rudy cranks the heat to full, and he tells a story about a hum-job from a hooker in a truck-stop bathroom. And another about a brawl with tire irons on the New Jersey Turnpike. And one more about something called Thai-stick that turns the meanest motherfuckers into gentle lambs and makes the whole world beautiful and full of love. "You know," he says, "it's all in how you look at life."

"Yeah," Mick says. "It's just your attitude, right?"

"That's all it is," Rudy says. "But hell, I don't really think I need to be telling *you* that." He laughs loudly.

They sit quietly for a few miles, comfortably exhausted, until Rudy digs his hand into a loose pile of eight tracks and comes up with something brand new to Mick – "This blind cat named Stevie Wonder!" And then he says, "I'm going to Baltimore."

"I'm going to Woodlawn," Mick says.

"Woodlawn? You're shitting me! I'm going to Woodlawn or through Woodlawn to Catonsville."

Three hours later, Mick stumbles out of the van, barefoot and bare-chested, onto his own driveway. He opens his front door to the fiercest lecture of his life. His father's glasses are clouded from perspiration. *Is that possible?* His father presses his thumb deep into Mick's skinny biceps. As he speaks, with his free hand he swipes at the back of Mick's head to underscore certain themes. Careless and thoughtless. Worried sick. Sick with worry. Broken mower. What's that smell? Things are going to change, mister. He shouts a list of the terrible things that might have happened, and though it is long and more detailed, it is not nearly as frightening as what Mick had imagined himself when he was tumbling under the surf or when he was about to step into Rudy's van.

Mick's mother looks at him with an expression that goes beyond disappointment. She says, "I thought I could trust you." She utters the all-too-familiar refrain. "Where did we go wrong?" And once more when she meets his gaze, her face full of pain and bewilderment, she says, "Who is this boy we raised? I don't even know him."

Mick hangs his head, not only to avoid the swiping hand of his father but because he feels guilty, confused, and lost. He wishes he could run, miles, years, forward, or back; it doesn't matter.

"There will be daily homework. Additional chores. No television. And there will be an eight o'clock curfew every night until the end of August. Do you hear me, mister?"

Mick nods.

"Do you have anything to say for yourself?"

"No," Mick says.

When Mick returns Donald's mower, Donald and Mrs. Hagner are sitting in her Impala in front of the house. Donald flips Mick the bird as they drive off. Mr. Hagner silently opens the garage. He inspects the mower and then stands and watches with his arms folded across his chest as Mick walks back toward his home. If only he could pass Barry or Terry on the street...

There's so much he wants to tell them, but the streets are empty, and his mother and father are waiting. No detours. No funny business, mister.

No one, after all, can rescue Mick's summer. It is going to suck big time. Gonzo suck. Suck it out the ass. Bite the mega schlong. *But* -- Mick survived his adventure. He even made a new friend, a black man named Rudy, who'd been to war and come back. He said with a fist bump and a laugh, "Take it easy, brother. Or take it any way you can."

Mick is 13. The year is 1977. People are talking about a band called The Talking Heads, a condition called Saturday Night Fever, and this brand knew cat named Luke Skywalker. It's as if a door blew open. Something entered. Someone departed. In spite of a dozen restrictions, one thing Mick doesn't feel – can't, won't ever again – is grounded.

A Likely Story

It's Sunday morning at Two Pines, and I am unpleasantly preoccupied as I am so often lately. It is quiet before the daily storm of bathing, grooming, and dressing. All but one of our eight residents lie in bed, though only a few are sleeping. Mrs. O'Rourke of room five has put a pan of water on the stove for her oatmeal. I know that because my lead counselor, Antonio, tells me after finishing his rounds. I've been sitting in the office reviewing charts.

"Is nothing, Mr. Norton," Antonio says. "You mind I do my training now?"

I shrug, uncertain.

"The First Aid video and multiple-choices test," he says.

"Now's a good time."

There are two desks in the small room. When Antonio sits before the computer monitor, we are nearly back to back in our office chairs. The door is open. I can hear but can't see Mrs. O'Rourke shuffling some fifteen feet away down a short corridor in the kitchen. We have one large window facing the street. The blinds are drawn. Occasionally, I hear the hiss of tires on the wet roadway. Or maybe the road is dry.

I appreciate Antonio for staying busy in productive ways unlike the other young staff who use down time to dote on the devices in the palms of their hands. I also feel restless, not uncommon lately. It is the middle of the month with no urgent need to prepare forms for billing. We recently had been audited, so I have a few corrections to submit and file. The prospect bores me.

Soon enough, the still surface of our morning ripples. I hear Mr. Pagano muttering and Mrs. O'Rourke's familiar breathless complaints. From where I sit, I can't distinguish the words. Whatever the discrepancy, it will probably whip up into a storm without some intervention. Mr. Pagano is fond of the phrase "filthy whore" – which is highly unpopular with the women in the house.

Antonio tries to stand, but I put my hand on his shoulder. "Stick with what you're doing," I say. I thought I might welcome the distraction.

Mrs. O'Rourke's is a tale of unusual pain. Within a period of six months, she lost her husband and her only son, but these are things of which we haven't spoken, not yet. Her rage this morning is for Isabella, our cook and shopper who has failed to buy the steel-cut oats on her last visit to the supermarket. I don't know if she has been talking to Mr. Pagano or to herself, but Mrs. O'Rourke tells me she had specifically requested the steel-cut Irish oats, and more, that she seldom asks for anything, and why should her single modest desire have been denied her. To which Mr. Pagano responds: "Ireland's for cock-suckers."

Naturally, I do not take Mr. Pagano's remark at face value. "Why do you want to upset Betty?" I ask.

He sits at the kitchen table, his quad cane leaning on his knee. He does not look at me. "The Irish are as bad as the Jews," he says. He gestures a man stroking his penis. Mrs. O'Rourke wipes her eyes, lets out a loud sigh, and drifts off into the pantry. My brief intervention was unhelpful, but I suspect another opportunity will present itself, probably within ten minutes.

While Mrs. O'Rourke is still out of the room, I kick Mr. Pagano's foot to get his attention. In the classic gesture, I say, "Up yours."

He lurches in his seat, coughing, wheezing, and laughing. He holds his false teeth in place with his fingers until he regains his composure. Then he returns the gesture with delight and says, "Watch your ass, Norton."

I've heard plenty of stories in my years at Two Pines. When exactly I wearied of the details and listened instead for only patterns and themes, I don't know. Perhaps it's easier to ask why than who and what and how and when. Perhaps it's pure instinct when a bent, old man like myself tries to get out from under the weight of useless information. Nonetheless, I've made a mental catalog, a distillation:

Woe is me; I'm everyone's fool.

I'm no one's fool (*watch your ass, Norton*).

No one appreciates what I go through (*but you'd better, Norton*).

Whatever happened to our joy, our innocence, and our youth?

Dear Norton, what a strange and marvelous world this is!

I've made other observations too. Plenty of stories tell us *this* is what men are and *this* is what women want. My generation is fond of the form: my people *X* and your people *Y*. To their credit, the youngsters seem less inclined to speak in such sweeping terms, but they say *like* so often. It's hard to follow the thread; a story seems more like a series of hinges.

A second ripple disrupts the fabric of our morning. I hear the soft-spoken, serious Antonio let out a cry from the office, "*¡Dios mio!*" When I reach the doorway, he says, "*¡Mi novia!*"

Many a tale – I've noticed – revolves around an uncanny coincidence. Whether rhyming events hold any special meaning I can't say, but it seems they often provide the motivation to tell. Maybe the experience of coincidence and events *as* a story are intimately bound. My own narrative is likely to challenge your credulity. Does it matter that you believe what follows? Again, I can't say.

I stand behind Antonio, looking over his shoulder. On the monitor, a young woman in pale green scrubs with a long, brown braid dials 9-1-1.

"Where is she?" I ask.

He points to the monitor.

"Yes, but–"

"*La Migra* took her. We was going to marry."

"I'm sorry," I say. "She's lovely."

He inhales and clicks the mouse. I think I should watch with him for a moment out of respect, sympathy. A graphic appears on the screen, reminding students of the three C's in case of emergency: check, call, and care. Next, we see the woman with the long braid tending to a silver haired woman lying flat on her back on the floor. The woman appears to be unconscious. She looks like…my deceased wife! I borrow the back of Antonio's chair for support as his dearly departed tilts my own onto her side. The nasal narrator emphasizes the need to support the head and neck.

Maybe coincidence is merely an illusion of pattern, or maybe it is evidence of an intelligent design, the hand behind the curtain. Though I had never seen her performance, I remembered Lynn telling me that she had volunteered to do some work for Red Cross – six years ago.

Sometime later, in the middle stages of Lynn's illness, she sat up in bed and gently brushed my chest through my pajamas. "Bet you didn't know you were sleeping with an actress," she said.

"I didn't know," I said. "I'm not sure what you mean."

"I play a dying woman." She smiled the smile that made me believe she was with me and always had been. All the rest was a bad dream. "You'll see."

Some other time – it's impossible to remember precisely – I had sat facing her with our knees touching, just as the pretty young nurse with the braid in the video sits before her, taking her pulse. Seeing the faint quiver in Lynn's lower lip, I could almost feel the soft silk of her wrist in my hand. She had been crying, which was not unusual at all back then.

"Are you frustrated, dear?" I asked. "Is there something I can do to help?"

"I'm leaving you, Reggie Norton," she said. "It has been a hell of a ten years."

I knew she wasn't joking. But given the state of her mind, her forgetfulness and confusion, and her vast and unpredictable mood swings, it was also difficult to take her seriously. We had been married forty years. "If you go," I said, "who can I count on to break my heart?"

"You can count on your own life to break your heart," she said. And then or soon after, she said something about a bad smell coming from the refrigerator, which had been one of her many obsessions toward the end of her days. She asked if I was going to put her in a nut house, which was one of her frequent fears. And, she said that she had always wanted to "sail on a ship across the ocean, to see the pelagic birds and the leaping dolphins, ever since I was a little girl."

That was news to me.

With coincidences and profound losses, we're apt to exclaim; *Everything happens for a reason.* I've heard it a million times. The following day, she left me. Not by ship but with a fistful of hydrocodone and a glass of white wine. I found her sitting on one of the Adirondack chairs beside the garden. Her chin planted in the crook of her neck. Her eyes closed.

Antonio cries out with tears in his eyes. "This shit is crazy, Mr. Norton. The way she hold the phone… The way she shake her hair… She look just like *mi novia*."

"But it is not her," I say. A question. A statement?

When exactly I wearied of details, I don't know. I wonder, as I've often wondered, if there was anything I could have said or done to change Lynn's mind. I decide, as I often have, probably not. But what about my own mind?

"Antonio," I say, "will you be okay?"

He stares at the screen, subtly tilts his head .

"For good or bad," I say, "we see the present through the past." I pat his arm. "Excuse me." I find Mrs. O'Rourke in the pantry, trying to collect herself in her way.

"Mrs. O'Rourke, why is the world so cruel to us?"

She narrows her eyes and turns to face a shelf of canned goods.

"Have you ever sailed across the ocean?"

She shakes her head.

"Please tell me about the Irish oats. When was the first time you had them? Who was with you? What color was the sky?"

What Do You Want?

Len:

Liz was born seven pounds, something ounces. No birthmarks. I was told that her birth was unremarkable, except that she arrived three weeks late. Even then, she was in no hurry to come out. She reached all her milestones on time or just a little behind the curve in some cases. She rolled from back to front and front to back. She was slow to smile. What made her smile was anyone's guess. When it came to speech though, she didn't say her first word until she was three years old. The babysitter said, "You've finished your milk, Little Lizzie." And Liz responded, "Apparently." There were several witnesses, significantly her father.

A month later, she finally got around to naming her significant others, her objects, her ma, and her da. She said "*mother*" accompanied by air quotes. And the following day, she said "*father*" and rolled her eyes.

Her first complete sentence was spoken to her mother but within earshot of her father. "*You* married him," she said. It came in the middle of a changing, and half a moment later, she asked, "Why *these* diapers?"

This much I've been told about young Liz and her family. We know roughly as much about baby Jesus and his parents. As with that story, we only get to know our subject around age thirty. Were there daisies or bucking broncos on her first-grade pencil case? Did some adult take off her bike's training wheels and run alongside with one hand on her seat and the other on her handlebars, cheering? Did some lust-driven teen fumble with the clasp of her bra? We can wonder if she played soccer or field hockey, had boyfriends, girlfriends, or both, smoked dope, aced her SAT, or spent a year at Pelican Bay. I don't know. Does the *W* tattoo on her shoulder stand for Women or Wittgenstein? Was she drunk when she got it?

Liz was a temp in an office on Market Street, downtown SF. As a bicycle messenger, I'd occasionally bring packages to that office. Upon first seeing her, I took an interest. It was her eyes maybe. Or the back of her head. I think it was her incredible self-assurance. She had something I wanted, but so do a lot of people I meet.

One wet Tuesday morning, I was exhausted from racing traffic. I had made a couple urgent trips uphill to Union Square. My knees ached. I remember thinking, *this can't be my life.* When I arrived at Liz's desk, she had been summoned away, so I flopped into her chair and listened to my pounding heart. Her phone rang eleven times before I decided to answer. There was a pen and notepad at the ready. I only wanted to help. Or that's the story I was prepared to tell.

The caller, like me, had never met Liz, though I at least had laid eyes on her. She introduced herself as the second wife of Liz's father. She'd had a hard time tracking Liz down, and she was almost breathless with excitement when she got me. The woman called to inform Liz of her father's death and to invite Liz to the funeral in Colorado.

Presumably she, the caller, had learned all she could about Liz from Liz's father. Before he had died, he read the unread letters from Liz's mother, written shortly before she died. On his deathbed, he had a few regrets. Bad investments. Useless diets. He had wished he hadn't tried so hard to quit smoking since in the end, it was a few bad mushrooms which undermined him. But most of all, he regretted abandoning his wife and little Liz back in NYC almost thirty years ago. Illness, it seemed, got him thinking about eternity.

Why the woman on the phone shared such details with me I have no idea. Maybe because I pretended to be Liz's supervisor. Maybe because I said *we* could not afford to spare Liz at such a busy time. Maybe because I insisted that she, the woman, was a fraud. It seemed she felt the need to prove her intimate knowledge of Liz. Of which, she had really none.

"What the hell are you doing in my chair, Package Boy?"

Those were the first words Liz said to me. As I said, I had seen her once before – that time she peered over the top of her book and pointed to a place on the corner of her desk for me to set down an envelope. She signed it and promptly spun away to face the wall. I stood a moment, admiring the swing and bounce of her hair, scooped up my receipt, and left.

Liz picked up the notes I'd scribbled from my phone conversation and turned her back to me once again. She wore a sleeveless top; thus, I saw the *W* tat on her shoulder in a font I didn't recognize. "Where did you get this information, Package Boy?"

I couldn't tell if she was angry or amused. Some of both I think. If half of what her father's second wife told me was true, she was a rare specimen and possibly dangerous. I mean, I don't think I could fathom a mind like that. Let alone the attitude.

My first impulse – I don't know why – was to tell it straight. "A woman called. I pretended to be your boss." And then I lied. "I can explain."

"I'm all ears, Package Boy."

"Please don't call me that."

"Why not, *Package Boy*?"

I'm twenty-two, but I look sixteen. There's a nerve there, and she was stomping on it. I gathered my resolve and said, "I could also *not* explain. What's it worth to you, Temp?"

I'm good at reading expressions. Whipping through downtown at near light-speed on a bike, I know when a driver is paying attention, and I know when a driver doesn't give a damn. Liz cared even though she tried to hide it. Her irises were blue, cold like the edge of a pane of glass, but a single muscle in her handsome jaw twitched. I had her. I thought.

She sat on the corner of the desk and crossed one slender leg over the other. She leaned in close. Her face was only inches from mine. "What do you want?"

I thought I might want to slap her. Or kiss her. I had already taken her chair and violated her privacy. Either seemed a reasonable next step, but I was suddenly overcome with shyness. It was that question – *what do you want?* – it always froze me up. "How 'bout coffee?"

"This is how you get your coffee?" She walked over to the small table with a coffee maker and poured me a cup. She set it on the desk in front of me.

"Your father died."

Again, a subtle twitch but nothing more. "That's not what I asked," she said. She paused briefly, biting down on the tip of her thumb. "Let's go." She swept up her handbag and started toward the elevator.

"Don't you have to tell your boss?" I said.

"I thought I just did."

Liz:

For what it's worth, Len was born prematurely – three months ahead of the plan. His first bassinet was made of glass. The first parents he knew poked him, measured him, and handled him with latex gloves. He didn't tell me. If he had said that, I probably wouldn't have believed him. I had an inkling though. He's small for one, but he has strong legs. His personality, like his body, is built from compensation, always trying to catch up. Trying to find any advantage he can to make up for his deficits.

The coffee we shared came in stemware and tasted like juniper berries. My idea. The plan was to get him talking and see how clever he really was. I'd get some facts, and then test their validity in the evening. The Internet is an incredible tool, of course.

"What's your name?" I asked him.

"Len."

"Short for Leonard?"

"It's not short for anything," he said. A little color came into his cheeks. This guy was a real piece of work.

"Len Smith?"

"Len Lipschitz." The look in his eye dared me to make a crack.

"And is delivering packages on a bicycle your raison d'etre or something like a steppingstone?"

He scowled.

Here we were, the two of us, out together on account of his leverage and bribery, but I could tell he wasn't having the fun time he had expected. People rarely do when they go out with me. I'm not sure why. One day, I'll brush up on my conversation skills. Or it could have been the inclement weather. Or maybe, as he said, his knees were aching.

In any case, I was developing a theory about Len. Two theories, actually. The first: he doesn't really want what he wants. He only wants to feel assured he can get it. It's all in the conquest. I've met a few guys like that. My research supported this hypothesis. Early deprivation, abandonment, foster homes, frequent change of schools, evidence of learning disability, special classes, and always the need to prove himself. Basketball was a fiasco. In wrestling, he showed promise until he pinched a nerve in his neck. I suspect he heard the theme song from *Rocky* like a tape loop in his head.

My second theory may not be so different from the first. It's a matter of degree perhaps. Len knows what he wants, and he wants it badly, but it doesn't exist. In my way of thinking, theory one and theory two amount to the same: a driven man on the road to misery. But in the second scenario, I find the guy a little more sympathetic.

As for myself, I have little trouble saying what I want. I want a sandwich with sun-dried tomatoes and grilled shitakes. I want time to pursue my investigations, involving the great thinkers of the Enlightenment Period. Now, I'm studying the life and work of Scottish philosopher, David Hume. Often, I want to be alone. When a partner, man or woman, asks me what I want, I'm ready. The trouble comes when they ask, "Liz, what do you really, *really* want?"

On cue, Len Lipschitz hit me between the eyes.

"Do you want to go to your father's funeral?"

He tilted his head. His dark hair was short by the way, except for a long forelock, a contrived looking thing. After he came in from the rain, it looked like a wet tail inching south across his forehead.

"Your making more assumptions than I can count," I said. "For example–"

"Do you want to go?"

"For example, you're assuming that the woman on the phone was telling the truth."

"Do you want to go?"

"And that the man was in fact my father. And–"

"Liz, do you want to go?"

"*Do you?*"

"I've never been to Colorado," he said.

Len:

We exchanged numbers. We met again for *coffee.* We discovered that we had very little in common. Liz was born late; I was born early. She was precocious, and I have yet to bloom. But we shared a desire to quit our jobs as soon as possible.

"It's a shame though," I said. "I bet your damn good at copying and collating."

"I'll cut you," she said. "I'll poison you." She laughed.

I think she liked me, but I wouldn't have been willing to put money on it. We slept together. Slept only. In her bed. After a night of planning our excursion.

If at first, she was reluctant to share her thoughts, once she started, she wouldn't quit. Though what she shared and what I asked about seemed rarely to bare any relation to one another. We'd boarded the Zephyr train from SF bound for Frazer, a small town in Winter Park, Colorado. "Zephyr," she told me, "is from Zephyrus, Greek god of the west wind."

"Does it matter that we are traveling east?" I asked.

"It's perfect," she said. "Into the wind's teeth." Precisely how she saw the journey.

"Why? Is there something you're afraid of discovering?"

She bit her thumb and shrugged. She told me about the history of Yoga, the future of fossil fuels, the problems with a representative democracy, and the likelihood of a fifty-ton meteor colliding with the Earth. Miles and hours passed, and I drifted to sleep with the sad thought that maybe I was lonelier in her company than I was alone. Then she shook me and told me about David Hume – even recited long passages from *An Enquiry Concerning Human Understanding* – and about her life's mission "to cast a shadow of doubt over all things seemingly certain."

"What are deductions," she said, "but the manipulation of inductions and inferences? What are inferences but guesses and beliefs? Just because the sun has risen every day of recorded history does not mean it will rise tomorrow. When the cue ball hits the eight ball, you will tell me that the eight ball travels according to some basic principles, what you call laws of motion."

"Yes," I said. "Everybody knows that."

She laughed. "Sometimes I wish I had what you have, Package Boy."

"And what is that?" It was early afternoon, and we were pulling into the station at Winnemucca, Nevada, which had the biggest sky I had ever seen in my life.

"Ignorance," she said. After a moment, she punched my arm. "Now, don't start sulking, Len. Ignorance is a good thing. Embrace it."

Liz:

I was alone.

Len slung on his backpack, stepped through the sliding doors of the train, and sailed away. It took me five minutes to pack my books, notes, and clothes into my suitcase. It took another thirty minutes to find him, sitting in the coffee shop of the Winners' Casino on Winnemucca Boulevard. Half an hour was enough time for me to ask myself why I had included him on my journey and why was I making this trip at all. One half hour lost and alone, roughly halfway to my destination, yet I felt farther away than when we'd begun.

What was I hoping to find? Both my parents were deceased, and I had barely any memory of them anyway. Could I say I was on my way to pay my respects to a man who never respected me? Or to hear the ludicrous account of my early years again from a woman who claims to have been his wife? Who never met me? As I say, I had time to ask the questions, but when it came to answers, my mind was as empty as the sky in the distance. I felt certain of only two things: I would not be here if it were not for Len and that I had no desire to carry on without him.

You see, I did know what I *really* wanted, and Len Lipschitz had it. Or depending on how you look at it, he *lacked* it, and I had too much of it. I wanted to want the way he wants!

I saw the back of him on a stool in perhaps the gaudiest coffee shop on the planet. He leaned in to take a sip. "You've come a long way for a cup of joe," I said, "but I guess I shouldn't be surprised by that."

He didn't turn around. "You've come a long way to find me."

"Another assumption on your part," I said.

"I see."

"You don't."

"Well then, I don't see. But I will pretend that I see because that would be embracing my ignorance."

The waitress shoved a menu at me. On it was a portrait of Sarah Winnemucca, also known as Thocmentony or Shell Flower, the Piute princess. It just so happens that she was a hero of mine back when I was in the business of collecting heroes. What did I know about her? She spoke five languages. She was a translator and dedicated her life to improving understanding between the Caucasian settlers and the native tribes. She was brave. There was an omelet here named after her.

"I've come a long way to find you," I confessed. It's not pleasant to admit when you're wrong, but it wasn't nearly so distasteful as I imagined it would be. "I admire you, Len."

He turned a half revolution on his stool to face me. His eyes were pensive, his forelock full-bodied. He was becoming handsome to me.

Len:

Sometimes persistence wins, you get what you want. But it seems that I've had almost equal success with resignation. I chose to walk away, and Liz followed me. Perhaps I could only have her if I didn't want her. Perhaps I didn't want her, but I still wanted her to want me. It was the story of my life, and it never made a bit of sense.

"Are you hungry?" she asked.

It should've been a simple question. I started crying.

She sat on the stool beside me and put her arm around my shoulder. "Len?"

"I'm here."

"I'm here too. But where?"

"The middle of nowhere," I said. It was just an expression.

"I think you're exactly right," she said. She seemed to brighten at the prospect, as if to be in the middle of nowhere was an accomplishment, something better than being east or west of nowhere. She offered a brief but effective appraisal of our careers so far: bike messenger and office temp. And she evaluated our journey, our objectives, what might be gained by attending the funeral, meeting the second wife, etc. "Are we a couple of fools, Len?"

"I guess we are."

"I think we're not."

She spun me on my stool until I faced her. She gathered the front of my shirt in her fists and pulled me closer. She kissed me. "Let's get a room."

I tried to be cool, but it wasn't in me. "Okay," I said. "Okay!" I pumped my fist.

"But first, you have to make me a promise."

"Uh oh."

"Hear me out."

"Okay. You have my attention."

"Once you've had me, you have to still want me."

With that, she studied my face. *Really* studied my face. She pulled on my chin, looked hard into my eyes, and turned my head left and right as if to inspect my ears. She didn't seem to need a verbal response, which was good, because I didn't have one. She let go of my chin and took my hand. She led me like a child through the cafe, through a gift shop, and into a lobby where we approached the front desk from the back side. A man in a straw hat and bolo tie turned to greet us.

Liz:

The room was my idea, but Len offered to pay. He's pretty sweet about things like that. He was a bike messenger, and I was a temp, so our savings combined couldn't have filled a cart with groceries. We met halfway, which is to say we went Dutch and no frills.

"Just a bed," I said to the man at the desk.

He looked Piute, maybe Shoshone. "Don't you want walls and a ceiling, too?"

We all thought for a long moment about his remark.

"I want to finish college," Len said.

It was the first that he had mentioned it. "I want an orange cat," I said.

"I want to rehabilitate my knee."

"I'll rub it for you," I said. And then I said something that I had never told anyone. "I want to learn to ride a bike."

"You're kidding."

"No one ever taught me."

With the key cards in our hands, we bid the clerk farewell and followed the carpet to the elevator. We began undressing each other on the way up. Len peeled off my shirt and asked, "What's the W stand for?"

There once had been a Winnifred, or William, or was it Wallace? Honestly, I couldn't remember. "What should it stand for?" I asked.

I knew what he'd say, and I was tempted to speak it before the word came out of his mouth. But why should I do that? His grin made me smile in spite of myself. "Winnemucca?"

Where's Willoughby?

I.

The little red light on the fucking coffee maker is on, but the fucker's not dripping. Why? *Fuck*! Sally curses all the time when she's alone, and she's alone almost all the time.

The fucking dog rolls in the compost and hops onto the fucking sofa. The fucking wind is strong enough tonight to blow a box of empty cans and bottles off the deck and scatter them around her yard. Mostly, Sally curses God and Graham, her ex. She sometimes wonders if Graham has become godlike in her monumental rage. Or has God become ex-like?

She calls her old friend Willoughby eight times between 10p.m. and midnight. He's fucking difficult to reach under any circumstances – no computer and no cell, just a landline which he says he only answers when he's in a rare mood to give money he doesn't have to people he doesn't know.

She calls him because he has called her every Sunday night without fail, ever since he had been diagnosed with Parkinson's. That was in April. Their conversations had begun at her insistence, because she feared he might be lonely and withdraw from the world; she couldn't have anticipated how much she would come to rely on those weekly chats.

She keeps calling, because it happens to be Sunday, October 8th. He lives in a cabin on a wooded hillside, several miles west of Calistoga.

At a quarter past midnight, she takes a deep breath and calls Graham.

"Where are you?"

It has been more than a year since they've spoken, and last time she'd vowed that it would be the last time. *We grieve differently,* he had said. *Why can't you accept that?* He was in L.A. then, grieving with a chick named Zoe.

"I'm home," she says.

"It's 3:15!"

"Where are you?"

"New York."

"I shouldn't have called."

"Wait."

"Take a look at the news, Graham. Call me back if you want. I'm not fucking going to sleep."

She ends the call and clicks on the TV remote. The fire is vast and spreading rapidly. In fact, there are many fires. She hears the names of neighborhoods, boulevards, and streets. The first footage shows Fountain Grove and then Bennet Valley. Black swirls with flickering tongues of orange. The camera pans and points at what appears to be huge, billowing clouds. The entire screen goes white. A crackling sound. Then back to the black sky and flashing emergency lights.

She sees maps and diagrams. Coffey Park is burning, flames leapt over the highway. These winds are called *El Diablo*, she learns. They are intense, but also familiar, seasonal. It's a new concept. Fires have names too. Sort of like hurricanes. Sort of like stars. But not at all like stars. These fires don't stay put, and no one seems to know where they came from and certainly not where they're going. How do they warrant the dignity of a fucking name?

Graham is back. Urgent. "Did you talk to Willoughby?"

Willoughby presided over their wedding. He is their only mutual friend since the divorce. They had met and fallen in love -- *fucking* fallen in love -- in one of Willoughby's once famous writing workshops. Sally and Graham had had a child too. A girl.

"No. We always talk on Sunday night!"

"I know."

"You know?"

"He told me you've been transcribing tapes for him, typing up his manuscript. It means a lot to him."

"He said that?"

"What he said is that talking with you means a lot to him… Hey, maybe he got himself out on time. Or maybe he was evacuated."

"Maybe not, Graham."

A brief silence. It's as if she can hear the words that he needs to suppress.

"I'll get a flight in the morning," he says.

"Why? What can you possibly do?"

"I have no idea," he says. "Call me if you learn anything."

"Graham."

"What?"

"Nothing… Thank you."

"Oh," Graham says. "Willoughby is his pen name."

"What's his real name?"

"I never asked. He never told me."

II.

Sally searches the Internet. She consults Nixle and listens to KSRO. She identifies three evacuation centers in Santa Rosa, but she has difficulty getting any answers on the phone.

He's 75 to 80 years old. He might be in a wheelchair. He might have only taken his walker. He's bald. Likes western wear and denim, that sort of thing. But he might be in his pajamas. What kind of fucking pajamas? I'm sorry. He goes by Willoughby, I think. He has blue eyes. A slight tremor.

Now, she's driving east on River Road.

His tremor was slight three months ago when she last saw him. When she last saw him, his name was simply Willoughby.

Morning light feels dusky, gray, and a mean yellow orb hovers in the haze. The taste of the air reminds her of a smoky fire at the beach, damp wood and seaweed. Something tickles the back of her throat. A long line of cars and trucks come to a full stop near Forestville.

"I'm at SFO," says Graham. "Still on the plane."

"I'm sitting in traffic too."

"Shit, Sally."

"Did you know the last story he sent me is called *Deus Ex Machina*?"

"My Latin is rusty," he says.

"It means 'god from the machine.' Really, it means a bad plot."

"Is it any good?"

"It's awful. I think it was meant to be awful though. Fifteen pages of romance and betrayal, a love triangle, real high drama, but then it ends suddenly when the man and two women are swept away by a Tsunami."

Graham laughs. "That's life, isn't it?"

Sally laughs too. "Life has a way ruining good stories," she says. "Bad stories too, I guess."

After half a minute of silence, he says, "Sally, you know, I wish–"

"I have a call coming in," she says. "Ring me when you get up north."

This sudden impulse to weep. Strange. It has been years. A doc at Kaiser had offered her something to 'help her get over the hump,' but she refused. The expression made her furious.

She curses at the cars in front of her. Then turns up the radio. Twelve fires. Dozens reported dead and many more missing. Zero percent containment. A list of neighborhoods which have been evacuated and others standing by. Breitbart News reported that the fire was started by an undocumented immigrant, and now the local sheriff says there is no evidence to support that claim.

But what's to stop these fucking fake stories, like the fires from spreading? The fucking mendacity! Highway 101 is closed. Mendocino Avenue is closed north of College. She had intended to start with the Vet's Hall by the Fairgrounds, but maybe she should try the Finley Recreation Center first. Soon enough, a man with a respirator and an orange flag sends her in that direction, southward and down an unpaved road between a pair of dry empty fields.

The last time she drove to the Finley Center was five years ago for swim lessons. Gabby was three in red trunks and a T-shirt, matching red water wings. She was husky and fair, full-cheeked like her father. She was already ill then, but with no indications. Nothing that could be seen without a CAT scan. Sally tilts the rearview mirror as if she might suddenly find her girl in the back, dozing in her car seat. Her chest heaves. She almost sobs but stifles it. She rolls down the window, breathes in burnt air, and rolls it back up.

III.

At Finley, the lot is nearly full. By the entrance, she sees an ambulance and flashing yellow lights that look pale against the hazy yellow sky. She sees a woman, standing on the curb lift her respirator to take a long pull on a cigarette.

There is commotion in the doorway. One man, flailing, shouts, "Todos!" Another tries to console him. Once inside, she sees a line of mostly elderly, and women with small children. The faces are white or brown, anxious or bored, or both. Many eyes are trained on small screens in the palms of their hands. At the head of the line, a man is taking information, jotting on a clipboard.

She suspects that she will not be permitted to enter. Who can she ask? She sees a man in a FEMA sweatshirt near a man and a woman with Red Cross badges. Each is engaged, answering questions and enunciating every syllable. She understands. They mean to project a sense of calm and order, but the slow, deliberate mannered speech has always produced the opposite effect in her.

Not always.

She finds a space on the end of a wooden bench, sits, and breathes. Occasionally, one of double doors swings open, and she hears the low roar of many conversations. She glimpses at the long rows of cots occupied by bodies and backpacks. When the door closes, nearby voices become distinguishable.

"I guessed something was wrong, because my dog was sniffing and sneezing. And, of course, the wind."

"Animals know before we do."

"They do!"

"We saw the flames coming over the hillside. Jack, my husband, put a few things in the SUV and pushed us all out the door."

"We were told to evacuate by the Fire Department."

"We weren't told anything."

"The kids wouldn't leave without the cat. It was terrifying. Tuxedo hid behind some boxes in the garage."

"I tried to rescue the old man at the end of our cul-de-sac. I banged on his door, but he wouldn't answer. God help him."

Sally is moved to do something, anything. She interrupts a woman speaking to one of the Red Cross workers. "I'm looking for someone," she says. "Excuse me. I'm looking for someone."

The Red Cross worker points to the back of a long line leading to another Red Cross worker. "You can give her the name, and she'll check the list."

"What if I don't have a name?" Sally says. "Can I go in? Can I at least look?"

"I'm sorry," the Red Cross worker says, "but I can't have two conversations at once." She points again to the back of the line.

Sally pulls her phone out of her back pocket. "I'm on the bridge," says Graham. "Traffic is moving now but who knows?"

"Oh."

"Any news?"

"Nothing."

"I think I heard Sutter had to send its patients elsewhere. Maybe Kaiser too. The thought of going into a hospital again... Sally, you there?"

Sally's mind is playing tricks on her. There are two Graham's speaking, like those before and after photos you see in magazines. The big fellow with the red beard and the huge laugh. The author of half-baked sci-fi stories and *time machines.* The super-kind critic. The generous man she fell in love with. And the other – the after – the clean-shaven one with a gym bag and vacant eyes. Always on the move. Only able to speak in platitudes.

Graham says, "I'll find out what I can and call you."

She puts the phone back in her pocket and sees that the nearest Red Cross is turned, looking the other way. The door swings open, and she bolts through. She scans the room. She's good at this after so many games of Where's Waldo. Where's

Willoughby or whatever his name is? She looks for a white Stetson, a bald head, a frail man on a cot. She looks for a deep red aura. She is surprised by a sonorous voice, much like her dear friend's, but instead it's an elderly volunteer announcing the delivery of coffee and donuts.

IV.

She's on her way now to the Vet's Hall but why? This venture feels as hopeless as was the search for an oncologist with a new opinion. The search for solace in so many glasses of Cabernet. Traffic is slow, but her mind is racing ahead.

What was Graham doing in New York? Why does it matter? What will she say to him? How will she be with him? What will she ever do without Willoughby? Yes, people grieve differently. Of course, they fucking do. She just couldn't hear it from the man she had chosen to share her life's path, the man who fled when she needed him the most.

Willoughby could say it. He said it all the time. In their Sunday evening chats, she used to unburden herself, starting with something like the fucking coffee maker or the foul-smelling dog, or the horrors in the daily news. But quickly – and almost unwittingly – onto deeper stuff. Her reluctance to go back to work in a classroom since Gabby's death. Her absolute terror at the idea of dating. Her sometimes crushing loneliness.

In fact, Willoughby said little on the phone. He'd pepper in a few questions, and he'd listen. Occasionally, he'd offer a quote from something he'd been reading: Yeats, Rilke, but lately he had been immersed in the biography of the Dalai Lama.

By Wednesday or Thursday, she'd find a cassette in her mailbox with his newest story… *Prince Bradford and the lovely Camilla, paddle out for the first of their board-sailing lessons as Lady Enid watches through binoculars from behind a divi-divi tree.*

Out of nowhere, a fifteen-foot wall of water arrives to wash away all their untapped nights and days...

"I think I can be there in an hour," Graham says.

"Where?"

"Wherever you'll be."

"I'm on my way to the Vet's Hall. Do you remember where that is?"

"By the Fairgrounds," he says. "Oh God. Do you remember the petting zoo?"

When Sally remembers her daughter, she tends to see her in her later stages, listless and hairless in a bed or at the treatment center receiving intravenous chemo. She remembers the mouth sores and the poor appetite. She remembers holding out a spoonful of soup or Jell-O and waiting with a smile pasted on her face. Why *this* should be the case, she has no idea.

Yes, she remembers the petting zoo. Gabby was robust and willful then with the intent on straddling a potbelly pig. A miniature goat was equally intent on eating the ribbon in Gabby's hair. She had a fit.

"Hey," she says. "I'm coming to a detour. I'd better pay attention."

She turns up the radio and learns of more neighborhoods being evacuated and a new list of refuge centers. Thousands of homes destroyed. Tens of thousands of acres, vineyards, and woodland. So much fuel after five years of drought. Tubbs, Nuns, Redwood Valley, Atlas, Cherokee, were once the names of communities. Now, and perhaps long into the future, they will be remembered as the names of fires, the burnt topography of chimneys and chasses and the charred black trunks of trees. *Those who need not be out*, she's being told, *should stay indoors with windows closed.* What about these crazy winds – calm for now – but El Diablo is expected to dance again tonight.

At the entrance to the Fairgrounds is Grace Pavilion, a large hall with a high ceiling. It's often used for banquets or exhibits, but it is now lined with rows of cots. To the left is a station for volunteers. Beside it is a large table with boxes upon boxes of chips and granola bars, Gatorade, and bottled water. She steps back to avoid three small boys racing past, kicking a tennis ball. Other than the children, most of those in motion are wearing name tags, either Red Cross volunteers, nurses, or social workers. Here are people of all ages and colors, snacking, sleeping, or poking at the ubiquitous smart phones.

She sees an old woman sitting, massaging her bare feet. An attendant arrives with a wheelchair and pushes the woman down a long aisle to an open door in the back where a sign says, 'Medical Personnel Only.' Sally follows, looking purposeful, like she knows exactly where she's going. Surreptitiously, she scans the rows of nylon and aluminum beds.

As she exits Grace Pavilion, she passes a volunteer, possibly a nurse, seated at a table.

"Wait."

Sally pretends not to hear.

"Wait!" Louder this time. "Where's your mask?"

"Oh. Where did I put the damn thing?"

The nurse reaches into her pocket. She hands Sally a folded white rectangle with elastic ear loops. "Try not to lose it."

She paces forward, one dreadful step after another. The sight of gurneys and bags of saline. The smell of iodine. These are the accoutrements of her worst nightmares. *Try not to lose it* becomes her mantra.

Here again. This small city is divided into communities. On one side of the building, people are treated for burns on the other, smoke inhalation. Thirty paces ahead, in a bed by the rear wall of the facility, she sees him. As she gets closer, she sees that he is attached to an IV and a cardiac monitor. He's taking oxygen through a tube in his nose. His eyes are closed, and he appears to be sleeping.

"Willoughby," she whispers.

Slowly, a smile comes across his face. "No one here knows me by that name." He's hoarse. When his eyes open, they are red and swollen.

Her eyes swell with tears.

"How did you get in here?" he says.

She's unable to find her voice.

"They won't let you stay," he says. "But I'm sure happy to see you."

She swallows. "I'll stay until they kick me out."

His lids sink to half-mast.

"How are you feeling?" she says.

"I'm not in pain," he says. "I feel lucky to be among the living."

"And did you lose your house?"

"Oh yes. Everything. I tried to save a few books and papers. Foolish me." He sets one trembling hand on hers.

"Graham is on his way," Sally says.

"I am twice blessed."

A doctor comes toward them, pausing briefly at each bed, checking vitals, and asking, "How you doing?"

"We better get to work quickly," Willoughby says. "I once knew this woman–"

"Wait," Sally says. "You have a story? It's only Monday."

"It's only Monday? Well, then you'll forgive me, because this is a short one."

"You knew a woman?"

"Her house was on fire. Blazing, ready to collapse. She was out somewhere, say the garden. No, not the garden. She'd have noticed. She was at the store, running an errand."

"Should I be writing this down?"

A long pause. He seems to have faded out.

"Willoughby?"

"She ran into the burning house to save her child."

"Oh."

"The house fell down around them. Neither made it out."

"Oh God. That's awful."

"But," he says, "something of a miracle." He smiles again. His eyes are closed. "The child was unharmed."

"I'm afraid I don't get it."

Again, he appears to have nodded off. Now, the doctor is at his bedside.

"Willoughby?"

The doctor looks at Willoughby. Then at Sally. "This man needs to rest."

"He's my friend. I'm here because–"

"You'll have to visit another time."

With that, a nurse approaches and leads Sally out of the hall.

V.

Try not to lose it, she tells herself, walking back through Grace Pavilion. She dodges a small army of volunteers with arms loaded with bags and boxes. All this urgency. All this energy. Is it love? Where do people get the strength? She's exhausted, hungry; she hasn't eaten all day. She wants a tall beer. She feels bewildered.

Wait. She stops to rest on the edge of a vacant cot. Wait. I think I get it. She sees in her mind a ceramic urn with ashes in it. The child is unharmed. The child is already dead!

When she steps back out into the open air, she sees a spectacular show of orange, pink, and magenta on the bellies of the clouds. To the west is a fiery, red sun low on the horizon. She had thought she had used all her prayers, but maybe she'll try again. One for rain. One for Willoughby of course. How many do you get? One for everyone.

Graham is coming toward her. He's as big as ever and wearing his red beard again. "Oh Sally," he says. He wraps his arms around her. It feels like a *before* hug. "They moved some patients down to Kaiser in San Rafael. I think we should try there." He's almost breathless.

"He's here!"

"You saw him?"

"Briefly." She points toward the medical facility. "They won't let you in. Not now, anyway."

"Is he okay?"

"He was in and out, you know, but he's there. He's still in there." Sally wipes her eyes.

"Oh." Graham sighs. "I'm so glad to hear that. I'll see him. Maybe tomorrow or the next day. Whenever I can. I'll get a room down on Santa Rosa Avenue."

"Could be difficult," Sally says, "under the circumstances." She pauses. How exactly does she phrase her question? "Don't you need to hurry back to New York?"

"No," he says. "I think I've had enough hurrying. Besides, there's nothing there for me."

"Oh?"

"I saw some old college friends, slept on their sofas. Pretty much just got in the way of their busy lives."

"Oh."

"Remember how all my stories had time machines? Remember Willoughby said, 'what's wrong with now?'" He laughs. "I guess maybe I don't believe in time travel anymore."

"Maybe I do."

Graham looks puzzled.

"My house smells like compost," she says.

"Oh."

"It's because of the fucking dog."

More puzzled. "I'm sorry to hear it?"

"And we'll have to go out for coffee, because the fucking drip thing is broken."

He smiles the smile that she remembers best.

"Hi Graham."

A Lucky Man

Kevin has not been enjoying the game of Jell-O in the backseat; the boys falling into each other with every curve in Highway 116, nor their shrill laughter. When the road straightens, it's quiet enough to hear voices on the radio. Another well-worn Saturday morning conversation about steroids and home run records to fill time before the day's games begin. But Ted, Kevin's son, tunes in, in his own way. He hears the word *legacy* and repeats it a dozen times, stressing the first syllable and then the last, until the word becomes an incantation and a meaningless utterance.

After a few moment's chewing on the brim of his baseball cap, Tanner, Ted's best friend, says, "Pull up your pants. I don't want to look at your ugly legacies."

"Dude," Ted squeals. "I don't want to look at your ugly, knobby-kneed legacies."

"You boys aren't making a whole lot of sense," Kevin muttered.

"Stay out of this, Dad."

"Yeah, Mr. Reilly."

"No one asked for your impertinence."

Impertinence, Kevin recognizes this as one of Ted's vocabulary words. "No, I don't believe anyone did," he says to the empty seat beside him.

Ted to Tanner: "No one asked for your incontinence."

Tanner: "Shut up, dude."

Ted, choking with laughter: "You shut up, dude."

And with that, they're back to headlocks, body-slamming, and punching each other in the thighs. Soon, they arrive in a lot by the ball field. The boys heave their canvas bags of gear up onto their small shoulders. Side by side, they walk toward the dugout where their teammates are swinging their bats or tying their cleats.

Kevin watches. The boys walk so close that they bump into each other every few steps. The boys love to be silly together. They love to be together. This is love. They're drunk on it.

Or Kevin is feeling sentimental? An affliction of late. If he watched longer, he'd see Tanner pick up his pace, eager to join his other teammates. He leaves poor, undersized, and uncoordinated Ted struggling to catch up, tripping and falling over his baseball bag.

Or Kevin is burdened by a malingering sadness? An atypical, malingering sadness. It wasn't too long ago that he headed out on a Saturday morning like this one but alone to visit a recent divorcee by the name of Lindsay for whom he'd installed a granite countertop. She had paid him for his labors and promised something extra when the job was done. Sometimes when he's driving alone, he thinks he can smell her shampoo.

One of the boys' parents pulls a wide metal rake across the infield dirt. Another parent lugs a cooler from the back of a truck. The coach, an old high school buddy of Kevin's, spreads a lime strip out to mark the edge of left field. He tilts his head up briefly. From the car, Kevin waves and points. He means to say that he hasn't forgotten about helping the boys warm up their arms. He means to say that he's sorry. It's a lot to try to communicate with your hand and face fifty yards away. In any case, the coach has his eyes trained back on the sea of grass between them.

Helping the boys warm up wasn't the only promise Kevin had made. Now, because he has put it off, he has roughly an hour to write a eulogy for his wife's Uncle Tim. The memorial service is scheduled at two, immediately after the baseball game. It's not a job for which anyone volunteered.

Kevin was chosen because in the final weeks of his life Uncle Tim insisted, "No church. No priest. None of that bullshit." Because Uncle Tim willed whatever was left of his estate after the settlement of medical bills and cremation to be awarded to Ted. (Even though it proved to be a negative sum, it had seemed a nice gesture at the time.) Because they would be holding the service at Kevin's home. Because the few remaining friends of Uncle Tim are either sick or crazy. Because Tim had been a house painter and Kevin had worked for him for a few weeks years ago while studying to get his contractor's license.

Because once, all those years ago, Kevin had said in front of his wife, Brenda, and her sister, Katy, and her sister's husband, Bill, "The old man can be a helluva sweet guy in spite of himself." They were stunned.

There's no point questioning the choice now. Yesterday, Brenda steam cleaned the carpet, scrubbed the kitchen tiles, and baked lasagna. This morning, she'll shop for flowers and for a couple jugs of wine. She will rent a large coffee maker, some mugs, some glasses, and some folding chairs from the caterer. Today is the dreaded day, and Kevin will write a eulogy, because Brenda asked him to.

Before Kevin and the boys left the house, Brenda hugged him. Her cheeks were hot and moist. She hugged and kissed Ted too and even hugged Tanner, which was unlike her. She folded and stuffed a sheet of loose leaf into Kevin's back pocket. "This might help," she said.

"Thanks," he said.

"It might help you understand why I can't do it."

"Oh?"

She turned away from him, pushing a magnet across the refrigerator door. "Never mind," she said. "Give it back to me."

“Hey,” he said. “I'll take any help I can get. I'm in new territory here.”

She said nothing. She pushed the magnet back to where it had been.

“Honey, we've got to go,” he said.

“Don't read it,” she called after him. “Promise you won't.”

From a distance, Kevin resembles George Clooney. Up close, one can see the knot on the bridge of his nose from an inside fastball his senior year of high school, and a chipped tooth from an on-the-job accident some years later. Still, he is what they call easy on the eyes, and he has an easy confidence. Men like him. Women like him very much. Children like him too. He conveys a sense of proficiency and good humor even when he doesn't know what the hell he's doing.

So, it was last week when he sent a dozen roses to the lonely divorcee and a card with the inscription; *They say the darkest hour… XOXO – K.*

He knows there are formats for eulogies. Templates. Blueprints. ‘We are gathered here’ for example. One could begin with that. A few minutes after noon, every seat in the coffee shop is taken. Maybe it's a blessing, because he’d prefer a whiskey anyway. Half a block south is Forestville Saloon. He has driven by but never stepped inside. Around sunset, there's often a small crowd of smokers beneath its blue and orange sign, and two or three choppers parked in front.

When Kevin enters, he nearly trips over a stool. In the back, a thin shaft of light leaks through what may be a kitchen door, and behind a dark curtain is a neon red glow. The carpet is ripe from piss and cheap air freshener. Or maybe the fragrance is wafting in from the bathroom, wherever that might be.

"May I help you?"

"Afternoon," Kevin says even though he can't see anyone.

"Is it already?"

The dim figure of a man appears before him, slightly hunched, with gray hair combed back and over like a meringue topping. At the far end of the bar, he hears a woman crying and another woman trying to console her. They sound like heavy smokers, perhaps in their fifties. They sound like they had cocktails for breakfast.

His eyes are slowly adjusting to the darkness.

The bartender lifts a bottle of Old Crow out of the well and pours a shot over ice. Kevin opens his backpack on the bar. He sips. He bites his pen. *We're gathered here,* he writes.

"Is that Brady?" calls one of the women. And before Kevin can answer, she adds, "You asswipe. You got some nerve."

"It ain't him," the bartender says, lumbering in the direction of the women. "Just take it easy."

"I'm sorry," the woman calls. "I'm really sorry."

"You sure it ain't him?" the other asks.

"Name's Kevin Reilly," says Kevin.

"You're probably still an asswipe. All men are–"

"I'm sorry! She's upset. She's upset for me. She's my friend."

"I'm just kidding you, honey."

"Don't pay any mind," the bartender says.

It's like the voices are coming out of a cave. Kevin tries to turn his attention back to his drink and the paper in front of him.

"I knew a Kevin. He was a pig."

"Now stop it," the bartender snaps.

"What are you going to do, Larry?" one of the women says.

"It's Lawrence now. Don't you remember?" the other says, cackling.

"Oh, oh, oh! *Excuse* me! What are you going to do, Lawrence? Going to hit me?"

The bartender busies himself, wiping glasses with a rag. Gradually, he drifts back down toward Kevin. "This place can be hell sometimes," he mutters under his breath.

Kevin nods, but his mind has tripped into a memory, his own hell. The scene couldn't have lasted more than ten minutes, but pieces of it replay like a tape loop during the least expected moments. He had gone to see Lindsay out of sexual frustration, and for her, it seemed the need to feel desirable and connect with someone, anyone. Maybe their needs were exactly the same, but before he could remove his trousers, she shook in shuddering, moaning sobs. It was the loneliest sound he had ever heard, and it got in him. He had stood beside her helpless until she gave him permission to leave.

He points to a red-rimmed curtain. "That a pool table back there?"

The bartender punches a key on the register and scoops quarters from the drawer. "First game is on me."

The plan now is to shoot a rack and think about Uncle Tim. Let the memories come and maybe some choice words will follow. The two men once shot a few games of nine ball and shared a joint and pitchers of beer after painting a new set of condos down in the valley. It must have been eight years ago. It had been a hurry up job, an exhausting week of ten-hour days. Kevin lead with the tape and sheets of plastic, followed by Tim with the sprayer, and followed again by Kevin with brushes and rollers. There had been little time for talk other than the grunted instructions from beneath Tim's mask. *Get me that. Move on down to six. Rinse these buckets.* At lunch, Tim would sit in his truck with his thermos and classic rock on the radio, while Kevin stretched out on the grass with a sandwich and *The Plumber's Licensing Study Guide.*

On the break, Kevin scratches. Waiting for the cue ball to roll back down into the slot, he hears the front door creak and new commotion on the other side of the curtain. *Don't you dare serve that bastard, Larry.* And in a low, tired voice, *Sit down.*

God help Brady or anyone who looks like him, Kevin thinks. *Maybe this Brady has done something to deserve a good tongue-lashing. But no good would come of it, not here.* He sips. He shoots. He gives his head a shake and tries again to bring his mind back to the task at hand.

Sit and shut your trap!

Or what? What are you going to do, Larry?

Larry does what he should've done fifteen minutes ago. He puts a song on the jukebox, some sentimental Willie Nelson thing.

Uncle Tim had worn a braided ponytail like Willie, only his hair and beard were gray without a trace of red. Five years ago, he was strong, and had tight, wiry muscles from his wrists to the base of his skull. He could tilt a twelve-foot extension ladder over his shoulder like it was nothing or carry two five-gallon buckets of paint up three flights of stairs. He must have been in his early sixties. Even then, he had a swollen belly, which was perhaps the first signs of the liver cancer that would be his demise. His face was creased, haggard like the country superstar, but he didn't share the singer's soft brown eyes.

Uncle Tim wasn't much for eye contact or any contact for that matter. Not then and certainly not after. In the intervening years, he rarely showed up to family gatherings, and when he did, he seemed uneasy, standing in a doorway. At a backyard barbecue, one'd find him examining a crack in the fence or a tree's dead limb. Somewhere along the way, he had to quit alcohol and presumably any of the other substances which gave him pleasure or relief. Kevin goes back in his mind to the night they smoked and drank and shot a few games. To the best of his memory, it was the last time Uncle Tim had talked.

That night, Tim professed his love of music, especially the old songs. "The ones that make you feel young," he had said, "and full of possibility. No one with a pulse can listen to 'Tupelo Honey' or 'Domino' or 'You Send Me' and not feel at least a little lighter. What could be better to lift your spirit?" After the games and the beer, they stumbled out into the parking lot and sat on the tailgate of Tim's truck under a starry August sky. Tim opened the cab and pulled a ukulele out from behind the seat. He strummed and sang a few tunes. This Tim seemed totally out of left field. He had been all business all week long, never even cracked a smile.

Gradually, Kevin joined in. Together their voices rose above the roar of the bullfrogs in the woods nearby:

If you ever, change your mind,
About leaving, leaving me behind,
Bring your, bring your sweet lovin'
Bring it on home to me

They were loud enough that a small crowd from the bar gathered in the doorway. When they had finished, someone clapped and someone else whistled. They were not Van Morrison nor Sam Cooke. They sounded exactly like a couple of drunken house painters, spent and well-spirited.

It was then after the crowd had gone back inside, Kevin patted Tim on the shoulder and thanked him for the work. Tim also told Kevin that he was a lucky man. Kevin had heard it before plenty but rarely given the remark much thought. If anything, it seemed a kind of diminishment, as if he hadn't worked for it or didn't deserve his good fortune.

He responded with the standard, "It's the life of Reilly, man. What can I say?"

But Tim seemed not to hear or perhaps he thought Kevin hadn't heard, because he persisted. "You're lucky to be healthy and smart and young. Lucky to be getting your contractor's license. Lucky to have such a good-natured boy, a really sweet kid. Lucky to have married a beautiful woman like Brenda. She was always a good girl, and she's a great woman and mom; I'm sure of that." He put his hand on Kevin's shoulder. "Life was hard on Brenda and Katy. I wanted to help out, but I know I wasn't much help." His words were not rushed, but they seemed to come from some kind of compulsion, as if maybe they had been bottled up for years. "Me and Rob, her dad, never got along that great. I blame myself. I was an idiot. I've made a fucking mess of my life. If I could go back in time... Well, you can't. You just can't."

The eight ball leans on the thirteen. The cue ball rests against the bumper. Kevin tips his glass again and gets nothing but a chip of ice. His paper says: *We're gathered here.* His watch says, *time's running out.* And what about Brenda's note? He digs the slip of paper out of his pocket and unfolds it on the pool table.

After Dad died, Uncle Tim came to help around the house. He cleaned the gutters, washed dishes, and cooked. I can't remember so well. It seemed to make Mom happy to have him around or happier because it was such a sad time. He took me and Katy to the park, to go fishing, and other things. He wasn't the sour old coot you met at our wedding or all those years after. The experience seemed to awaken something in him.

Something good but something else too.

He came into my bedroom at night, a few nights. And Katy's too. Just once, *she said. He put his hand between my legs. He wanted me to tell him how it felt. I couldn't. I couldn't say anything. It felt like my dad was gone, and there was no one left to protect me. It felt like the world was a sinister place, like any expression of love was a lie, a cover for something else.*

It's a sickness, Kev, I know. I've tried to forgive him, but I don't know if my heart is big enough.

Kevin puts the paper back in his pocket. Something had gone bad after their father died. Brenda and Katy do not talk about that time. He had also known his wife and wife's sister held a low opinion of their Uncle Tim. The man had had trouble with booze, and there had been suspicions of meth addiction as well. Some kind of run in with the law too, but he didn't know the details and hadn't cared to know. As for incest – if that's what you'd call it – it had never even crossed his mind.

He passes through the curtain and sets his empty glass on the bar. One of the women is weeping, and the other pats her hair and coos, "He won't hurt you again, honey. I won't let him."

Kevin feeds a dollar into the juke box. "Pick a few songs on me," he says. On his way out the door, he hears, "Whoa, big spender!" and "Thank you honey! That's so sweet."

The brightness of the day is painful, disorienting. The day itself has been disorienting. One whiskey was too little and too much. Soon, he's driving. He's thinking. Brenda with her russet hair, her big sea-green eyes, and long slender neck. She hadn't had any significant boyfriends before she had met him; it's something he had often wondered about. He knows she loves him, as well as one can, but he has also always felt a kind of reserve from her when it comes to intimacy and sex. Her reserve gave a feeling of conquest to their courtship, that he was chosen and the lucky one. Though, in fact, there were no other suitors.

In the years since, it has been a source of frustration and loneliness. When at last he looked outside of their marriage for sex, he experienced loneliness like he had never known. Now, he longs only for simpler preoccupations, a lighter heart.

Those remarks from Uncle Tim five years ago, inspired perhaps by the beer and a sense of friendship, now seem like they might have been some vague attempt to apologize. Of course, Tim could not have known how much Kevin knew. Perhaps he had even forgotten what he did all those years ago. Or maybe he was attempting to conjure a story he could live with. That he could die with? It's all way too much as Kevin rolls into the lot by the ball field.

The game is over and two other teams have taken the diamond. Kevin wants to say a few words to the coach, but he has liquor on his breath, and he'd rather his old buddy didn't know it. From across the bed of the pickup, he utters, "Sorry, I missed the game. Lot on my plate right now."

The coach lifts two buckets of baseballs into his truck. "It was a stinker," he says. "You didn't miss anything."

"Still," says Kevin, "I would have–"

"Work on grounders with Teddy. Glove in the dirt."

"I will."

"It doesn't come easy for him like it did for you." The remark is part of an old and tired conversation from a man who has loved baseball all his life but didn't make varsity.

Kevin nods. "I get it." When he turns, he sees the boys in the backseat of his car. Tanner looks glum. Ted is eating cheese-flavored goldfish from a small bag.

"What happened?" Kevin asks.

"I think we lost," Ted says.

"You think?" says Tanner. "You *think?*"

"I think they broke our legacies."

Tanner turns away from Ted and faces out the window.

"Maybe it's time for a new word," Kevin says.

They drive the long straight stretch through the vineyards and the curvy part under the redwoods.

"Why weren't you there?" Ted asks Kevin.

"I had something I had to do."

"Did you do it?"

"Nope."

They ride on in silence. Tanner moping, Ted screwing and unscrewing the cap on his sports drink, Kevin rummaging through memories, feeling the first prickly sensations of panic. They drop Tanner off, and a minute later, they're rolling down their own street. Kevin recognizes Bill and Katy's silver Accord in front of his house, but there are more than a dozen other cars that he has never seen before.

Katy had been elected to spread the word since Kevin and Brenda would be hosting. She had said that she'd announce the memorial service in the newspaper and call a few acquaintances, mostly names that she had found in the guest book at the hospice where Tim spent his final weeks. But Katy and Bill smoke a lot of dope, and neither is good at following through. Kevin had no idea what to expect for the turnout. He and Ted sit in the car in the driveway.

"If Uncle Tim was Mom's uncle, what was he to me?"

"I don't know what you'd call him. Great Uncle?"

"Where is he now?"

"In the urn on the mantel."

Ted looks puzzled.

"He was cremated. That's what he wanted."

"So, all that's left is ashes?"

"Yeah," Kevin says, "and our memories of him."

"I remember he pushed me on the swing one time."

"Do you?"

"And how bald he got from the cancer."

"From the radiation."

"Oh yeah. The radiation."

Kevin exhales, which is something he seems to have forgotten to do all day.

"He used to do a trick that made it look like his thumb was coming off," Ted says.

Kevin unbuckles his seat belt and claps his hands on his thighs. "Better get cleaned up," he says. "The tan pants look nice."

In the doorway, Katy embraces him hard and whispers, "God, I'm glad to see you." Bill throws an arm around his shoulders and shakes his hand. The handshake is firmer than usual. He can't remember the last time he saw his brother-in-law in a tie and jacket. It's a Saturday. He should be in an apron with a pair of tongs in one hand and a beer in the other, but then nothing is as it should be.

Kevin sees a number of strangers, men and women, middle-aged and older. Some are sitting on the sofas, and others are on folding chairs. Some are eating lasagna from plates on their laps. Others are sipping coffee. Others are just sitting. No one is talking. No one is drinking the wine.

He introduces himself, and nearly in unison they say, "Hi Kevin."

He backs into the kitchen, followed closely by Bill and Katy. Brenda twists a dish towel over the sink. "You're late," she says without turning around.

"I have five before two."

"Well, they're early. They've been here for over an hour!"

"*Shhhh,*" Kevin says.

Katy gulps. To Brenda, she says, "I told you it's my fault." To Kevin she says, "I thought it was meant to start at one. I'm so sorry."

Brenda tosses the rag into the sink. She sighs and turns, but she will not look at Kevin's face. "Where's Ted?" she says.

Kevin embraces her – or tries to – but she turns away from him again. Is it because of the note? Does she feel exposed? Could she possibly know about the divorcee? Anything is possible. Is it because all men are asswipes? Pigs?

He looks at Bill as if to test the assertion. Bill looks like Bill: a little more bewildered than usual. If Kevin ascribes certain characteristics to Bill, like uncontrollable lust, the willingness to exploit someone who is vulnerable and frightened, or dishonesty, then indeed asswipe and pig seem fitting, generous even.

Brenda shouts. "Where's Ted?"

The kitchen itself bristles.

With her face tilted to the floor, she says, "Let's get this damn thing over with."

Kevin paces down the hall in search of Ted. He's not in his bedroom; he's sitting on the lid of the toilet seat, still in his baseball pants. He appears to have been staring at the faucet. "I like to watch the drops get swollen and fall," he says.

"I remember doing that," Kevin says. He smiles. "It's time, kid."

"I didn't change my clothes."

"Don't worry about it."

Kevin leads Ted back into the living room. He makes a quick detour into the kitchen, pours himself a juice glass to the brim with wine, and downs it in three swallows. He wipes his mouth with the back of his wrist and takes his place in the front of the small crowd. On the left are Katy and Bill, hands folded, and heads tipped forward as if to pray. To the right is Brenda standing among these strangers. Her hands clasped below her waist. She has Ted's freckles, or of course his freckles come from her. Her eyes are brimming, but the set of her jaw looks more like rage than sadness.

Kevin clears his throat. "We're gathered here," he says.

He surveys the room. Fifteen including his wife, sister-in-law, and brother-in-law. Sixteen with Ted, who is now parked against his mother's hip. Seventeen, counting Uncle Tim.

"Here we are...gathered," Kevin says. "To some of us, Tim was family. I imagine some of you knew him in other capacities." He pauses. What he has just said is so amazingly fucking stupid that he wants to run out the door, but he sees Katy and Bill nodding encouragement and others listening with what looks like anticipation. "Tim was a house painter. He was surprisingly strong. A lot stronger than he looked." Kevin closes his eyes. "He liked to fish. And he hunted some, back in the day. I think he hunted. He could play the ukulele... I guess I barely knew him."

Mercifully, a large man standing beside Brenda offers, "I met Tim in A.A." A woman standing behind Katy says, "Me, too." And then a voice from near the back says, "I met Tim in Narcotics Anonymous. What he shared is confidential, of course, but I think I can say he was brave. He was facing his demons." She nods at her own words. The large man nods. Another woman says, "Hear, hear."

"To his demons," Kevin says. "I mean, facing his demons." He risks a look at the half circle of faces in front of him, and he remembers trying to stand at the plate shortly after having had his nose broken by a pitch, of fighting an impulse so deep, so strong, to pull away. "To all of us facing *our* demons…that we might find the courage."

He sees Katy looking sideways at Bill, who is looking down at his own feet. Now, he locks eyes with Brenda. She gives her head a short, brittle shake as if to say: *Don't go there. Don't you dare.* He lets his gaze fall on Ted.

"Tim could make his thumb disappear," Kevin says.

Deadly quiet.

Bill says, "We'll miss him."

Katy says, "I'm sorry he had cancer."

"Amen to that."

"I'm grateful for his generosity," Brenda says with a warble in her voice. "He was alone, and he didn't have much, not anything, but still he wanted to leave something for Ted."

"Amen."

"He loved music," Brenda says. "We should say that."

"He did," Kevin says. "He really loved music." And after another uncomfortable silence, he said, "I'm sorry."

"Amen."

Bill and Katy do not linger after the ceremony. All the guests have gone, and Kevin is making himself busy by folding chairs and bringing dishes to the kitchen. He washes, rinses, and stacks, and in spite of it all, he can't stop ruminating over the events of the day. Uncle Tim had called him lucky, and he thinks it is true. Or it *was* true. He feels lucky when he thinks of his old high school buddy now coach, the pretty divorcee, or the weeping women in the bar. He's lucky when he compares his life to Brenda and Katy, who were so deeply wounded as children. He is luckier than Uncle Tim and luckier than Brady, or whoever the fuck that guy is. But he feels his luck may have changed, that the full weight of life is about to settle on his chest.

He's looking for something else to do when Tanner bolts through the front door. Ted had been lying on the sofa face down, kicking his heels in the air. Suddenly, he's up, renewed. Lucky Ted.

Brenda hasn't spoken since the memorial service, and Kevin hasn't wanted to intrude on her thoughts. She retired to the bedroom half an hour ago. She has just got out of the shower, sitting in her soft chair in her white terrycloth robe with a towel wrapped around her head, turning the pages of a magazine. That's how Kevin finds her when he comes in search of his reading glasses.

"Some eulogy," she says without looking up.

"I couldn't think of anything to say."

"That's not like you."

He nods.

A pause. "Someone named Lindsay called. I forgot to tell you. She sounded... I don't know. Sad."

He nods again.

"Is it important?" Now Brenda looks up. Her eyes are clear; her jaw relaxed. She looks at Kevin like she's seeing him for the first time after a long time apart.

"I don't know," he says.

She closes her magazine and sets it on the nightstand. "Are you crying?"

He shrugs.

"Sad for me, Kev?"

"For you," he says. "For us."

She smiles. "Where's Uncle Tim?"

"I put the urn in a box. It's on a shelf in the garage."

"In the garage. That's good. Think the boys can put themselves to bed?"

"It'd be a first," he says.

"Well, it has been an unusual day."

He nods.

"Why don't you sit?" she says.

He sits on the bed. She clicks off the lamp and stands in front of him. She unwraps the towel from her hair, peels off her robe, and lets it fall to the floor. She clasps her hands around the back of his neck and pulls, pressing his forehead into her bare belly. The scent of her soap. The scent of her. As she does, she hums an old soul song. Nothing could be better to lift the spirits.

Rage, Rage

Six hours ago, Dad's second wife, Dorothy, was laid into the ground. I don't know what went wrong, only that nothing went right. The man who gave the eulogy wore a captain's cap and made numerous references to sailing, seafaring. To my knowledge, my stepmother had never been on a ship. She came from Nebraska and resettled here in Maryland at the ripe age of 65. She met my father in a class called The Next Great Depression at OLLI, which is somehow short for Osher or the other way around. Before she lost her wits, her major passion had been the garden with a minor in gnomes and bird feeders. Maybe she ventured into hydroponics? Aquatic fertilizers? I didn't know her well.

Dad had made all the arrangements, and the moment the services began, he let out a howl and stormed off. I found him sitting in my rented Nissan, fogging the windows. He has been silent ever since, so I say as much on the phone to his sister, Aunt Bobbie, who's in ICU because of the kidney, the blockage.

"What?" she says.

"He's livid."

"What?"

"He's pissed. Beyond pissed."

"Lucky him," she says. "Wait. Do you mean he's drunk?"

"What's that noise? I can barely hear you."

"The groaning is from the machine with the pump. Or maybe *This Dying Light*. It's one of my shows. Is that salmon? Poached chicken? How come it's pink?"

"Aunt Bobbie?"

"You mean he's pissed off," she says. "Of course, your father's angry. He has every right to be angry. Put the lid back on. Push it over there."

"He's more than angry," I say.

Mild-mannered Dad, on a short night of sleep, could be curt. He could be cranky. He could be sarcastic. But nothing like this. When he became Dorothy's primary care, he was nominated for best supporting. They were like Siamese twins attached in the desire to keep her satisfied. When she wanted to see the old wooden carousel from her childhood, that was their plan. Never mind that the carousel and the little town in which it resided had been paved over decades ago. Never mind that she was in bed with a broken hip. "I'll ride the elephant, and you ride the purple pony," he had said.

"Aunt Bobbie, this is different. I've never seen him so incensed."

"You're the therapist. Am I right? What do you think?"

"Anger is one of the five stages. Stage one. Or maybe two."

"He didn't die. She died. No, I won't eat it."

"That's my point. He should be–"

"Grieving? You're still a child, Lloyd."

"Well..."

"I love that about you. You don't have a clue. How old are you?"

"Aunt Bobbie, he's grieving the loss of $11,000. He hasn't mentioned Dorothy since I came home."

"Just give me the Jell-O," she says. "Christ, I haven't had Jell-O since I was seven."

"Aunt Bobbie?"

"All I eat here is Jell-O."

I watch as Dad fills in the Tranquil Meadows Customer Satisfaction Survey with his red pen. Was visitation carried out as planned? No. Were you greeted within two minutes of arrival? Fuck no. Were the costs for services made sufficiently clear? Fuck. Did you experience any problems? He stands and swings his quad cane at the overhead lamp. He falls back into his chair.

"Dad," I say, "do you want to talk to Aunt Bobbie?"

"Why?"

"How about Uncle Frank?"

"The fucker's in Mexico."

"New Mexico."

"You want to know what I want?"

"That's why I'm here, Dad."

He looks at me the way Dorothy looked at me almost three months ago, the last time I visited. I sat on the chair beside her bed and held her hand. She said, "Fill it with unleaded and check the oil, honey."

"Dad, it's me. Lloyd."

"I know who the fuck you are. Do you know who the fuck I am?"

"I'm not used to–"

"I want to get what I paid for. Do you understand? I want to settle up. Even fucking Steven. Nothing less."

"Well," I say, "the service was pretty odd."

"Odd," he says. "Fuck odd."

"There must be some explanation." Maybe Dad's mouth is dry. It seems that his upper lip is stuck in an unusual position.

"There must? Must there?"

I sit beside him at the dining room table. I give him my patented listening face.

"Tell me what you do again."

"MFT," I say.

"I know what MF stands for, but what's the T?"

"Marriage and Family Therapist. I help people–"

"You're not very good at it," he says. "I'll bet I can guess what you're thinking right now."

I don't see any point in arguing. This new Dad is not entirely unprecedented. Some familiar tendencies are amplified to the max. He'll make a guess. I'll deny it. He'll insist that he's right. That he knows me better than I know myself.

"You're thinking where the fuck's my little sister, Sally?"

He's right. I need Sally. Even though I know she said she was going back to the hotel to get a little sleep, I'm thinking where the fuck is she? She's a moderate, a model of compromise. Dad trusts her. She married into Pest Control, and she has done well for herself. "It's honest work," he had said before. "It's useful."

"You're thinking where's Sally, so I can get the fuck out of here and have some fun. Why are you going over to Timmy's? You boys want to run naked through the woods?"

"That was almost forty years ago, Dad."

"Well, it nearly killed your mother," he says. He's referring to my mother who died from cancer when I was nine years old. Sally was three then, so she doesn't remember Mom at all. Dad never mentions her, and on the rare occasions I've brought her into conversation, he's become quiet, distant.

A cloud passes through the room; shadows sweep across his stone jaw. The color in his non-milky eye goes from blue to gray. I think the conversation might have reached its end. Boris, Dorothy's Corgi, brushes against my ankle under the table. The digital on the sidebar clicks to 6:00.

"I'll tell you what else you're thinking," he says.

"You're batting a thousand," I say.

"You're thinking that this is just a stage he's going through. One or maybe two, right? You're not the only one who has ever read a book."

"Well," I say, "grief is natural under the circumstances. It takes many forms."

"Is that what the fuck I'm feeling?"

Sally and I got a double room at the Days' Inn across from the Knights' Inn on Security Boulevard. She said the Knights' Inn has rodents. She pulled a glue trap from under one of the beds. Sally drove down from Buffalo, and I flew in from the west, Berkeley. Dad has lived in this Baltimore suburb for almost sixty years. It's where he and our Mom bought their first and only home. They put down roots when he was hired at the Social Security Administration, the headquarters, right here in Woodlawn. He says he pushed a mountain of paper and for what? His knees hurt. He says the property value climbed steadily for half a century, but now it's in the basement. The basement's toilet. "White flight," he had said. "Like you kids. You flew away."

Five years ago, we had each offered to help Dad and Dorothy resettle in upstate NY and California, respectively, but he always said no thanks or no way or too cold and too flaky. Respectively.

"What about Dorothy?" we'd ask.

"She's already disoriented. What do you want to do to her? Besides, we're Ravens fans. And we like crab cakes even though we can't eat them anymore. We like being near them."

Sally says that she doesn't mind that he lies since everyone lies. She just wishes he'd try a little harder.

It took Sally ten rings to pick up. "Were you sleeping?"

"I was on a swing on a boat. The boat was in the sky. I was eating cake."

"I'm sorry."

"How's the angriest man alive?" she asks.

"Stable. He says he wants to get even. Even Steven. I don't know what the hell he wants."

"If Dorothy had said that, we'd say, 'Of course you do' and give her an orange popsicle."

"It worked."

"Well, I don't think I'd say it to Dad."

"No."

"He's just as crazy."

"Do you think so?"

I peek from the kitchen and see Dad still at the dining room table with Boris on his lap. He's mumbling obscenities.

"Sally?"

"No," she says. "I don't think he's crazy. He's angry, and he has been angry for years, but now he has no reason to pretend otherwise."

I'm impressed. I might have said something about care fatigue and isolation or feelings of impotence in a world that's become incomprehensible, but her analysis seems as good as any I could've given. What are they teaching in pest control these days? "He says he wants to know what you're driving."

"I don't understand."

"He said my little Jap thing won't do."

"I still don't understand."

"Neither do I," I say.

"You know what I'm driving."

"Of course."

"Did you tell him?"

"No." I say. "Hey, I better look after him."

"Are you hungry, Dad? Maybe you should eat."

"I could go for a beer," he says.

"How about something to go with it?"

"Sure, get me a coaster."

We're on the sofa, and he holds the remote in his fist. He clicks back and forth, a documentary about cannibals vs. the Republican presidential debate. Now, I'm counting blue ties and red ties, drifting in and drifting out. We're both waiting for Sally to come by in her pest control truck. That massive thing with a crew cab, a big wooden hammer hovering over the head of an unsuspecting mouse painted on the side. She had said, "Ordinarily, it's got a variety of poison in the back," but she takes all that out for family events. I asked Sally how roach poison works, because, well, she seemed a little down. She likes it when I show interest in her job.

"Which one?" she smiled.

"Which one is your favorite?" I asked.

"Hydramethylnon is a slow acting stomach poison. They eat it, get lazy, and die. If another eats the carcass or the feces, they die too. Voila. Fipronil disrupts the central nervous system. I remember when all we used was boric acid." She sighed. "Some days those were."

A heated exchange brings my attention back to the set. One's a loser, one's a liar, one's too fat, and one appears to be sleeping. Alas, in spite of all the vehemence, they find some common ground.

"Every one of these guys wants to get his dirty mitts on Social Security. What's that all about?" I ask.

"Fuckers," Dad says beneath his breath. He switches it back to the actors playing cannibals in cannibal costumes. The screen goes dark. Occasional flickers of firelight. Something turning on a spit.

"She called me Micky," he says.

"Who was Micky?"

"I guess I was."

I think I see a tear in his un-milky eye.

I could say that Dorothy once called me Micky, but that might only make him feel worse. I could say that after eight long years of your seeing to her every need, in the end, she didn't even know your name. Life blows, I could say.

After birth, it's all downhill, a succession of losses. Maybe it starts going south at conception. Ask me about Linda, my ex, who left me when her book, *The Unfillable Hole,* made the NY Times bestseller list. She relocated to the high rent side of the bay to give motivational speeches to the start-up geeks. She shacked up in a million-dollar shack with one of my sex-addicted clients.

I don't know what to say, so I employ a therapeutic silence. Under the circumstances, I think sadness might be better than anger. Let his words linger; let the tonal shift resonate. Let's have a moment of... Let's have a moment. But suddenly, we're competing with the shrill Australian narrator, and he is competing with the pounding of a dozen goatskin drums as he explains how the brain is cooked inside the skull, served hot. Dad clicks off the TV.

"She had a few lucid moments in her last days."

"I didn't know." What I know is that the beer seems to be helping. "What did she say?"

"She said she wanted to be buried on the top of a hill under a Japanese split leaf maple."

"That's fairly specific."

"Fairly fucking expensive too."

"I didn't see any–"

"Of course, you didn't."

Call it jet lag even though my flight was two nights ago. Call it grief stage three point five. Vicarious grief. Secondary grief infection. The funeral services were bizarre, for sure, but most of what I felt was pure boredom like I was on a school field trip to the DMV. There was a twenty-five-minute wait behind the hearse. The man in a dark suit, the funeral director I assumed, waved our small procession onward. There was a bit of commotion as men in coveralls erected a canopy and unloaded metal chairs from the back of a truck. I thought it slightly odd that the backhoe was parked just thirty feet from the gravesite. A man appeared from behind a tree with a cloud of cigarette smoke around his head, his captain's cap. And the music...well it was nothing Dorothy or Dad would have chosen. He listens to Rachmaninoff, and she preferred Italian opera. What we got was "The Wreck of the Edmund Fitzgerald" on a scratched CD.

I wanted it to end.

"You're angry about the maple," I say. "You should be. You have every right to be."

"Who's angry?" he says, blood beating in his neck.

"Well, that's good too. Being angry is okay and not being angry... Maybe that's even better."

"Thank you very much," he says. "Asshole."

"I only meant to say–"

"I have a plan," he says.

Suddenly, the sound of steps on the steps.

"Must be Sally," I say.

"It's not Sally. I know those fucking loafers." Dad tilts until his head hits the sofa, until his silhouette can't be seen through the sheer curtain at our backs. "Get on the floor."

I get on the floor. Next, we hear the loud crunch of an emergency break.

"Fuck," Dad says. "That's probably Sally."

"I brought escalloped potatoes," calls the voice from the porch. Four words dripping with condolence.

Sound of truck door shutting. Leather soles scraping on the brick walk. "You are so kind Mrs. Fitch."

"It doesn't appear anyone's home."

"They're here," Sally says.

"Fucking fuck," Dad says.

"I'll tell her that you're not feeling well," I offer.

"Tell her I'm lactose intolerant while you're at it."

But they beat me to the door, Sally first and Mrs. Fitch right behind with a casserole dish in her crab-claw oven mitts.

"Oh, poor honey," Mrs. Fitch says.

My father rises to his feet. He's not un-fit for eighty-three, but his balance is suspect. He rides the floor like a surfboard. I'm eager to see if he will shift gears and play the role of a sad widower as expected. It'd be a sign of ego strength. Or maybe he'll punch Mrs. Fitch in the stomach, potatoes and cheese bouncing off the cream-colored carpet.

Instead, he reels right past her to the chairlift on the stairway. He sits. Boris charges from beneath the table and makes a heroic leap onto his lap, ears tall and proud. With the flex of his thumb, the machine whines, carrying him to the second-floor landing. He lets his thumb off the gas and from his chair in the sky, he asks, "Got any shovels, Mrs. Fitch?"

"Call me Lucy."

"We need shovels, Lucy. And something with wheels on it."

I was fond of Dorothy. Dot, to her friends. Dot Zicker. All the motherly things she did, she was, even though she never had children of her own. The way she said *Lloyd* and put her silky hands on my cheeks. The way she made Dad laugh. Her garden. Her gnomes and feeders.

I had seen her only three, maybe four times, before the onset. I only remember us being alone together once at a restaurant when my father excused himself to use the can.

"He's so handsome," she whispered to me. "He's so romantic. That man." She shivered.

I felt somewhat ambivalent about this impostor, this sulky child who had come to inhabit my stepmother's soul. I wasn't so sad to see *her* go. The sadness I feel now is reserved for my father. Or is it worry? Or is it something else?

Truth is, I don't know what I'm feeling, and I often feel this way. Something happens on my walk to the Fitch residence. I'm doing my Emotion Cognition Inventory, and the mechanisms are mysteriously recalibrating. There he sat on his throne above our heads, angry as a pincer but dignified. He seemed – can I say this – self-actualized. He was like some super irate Gandhi or a pissed off Dalai Lama if you could imagine. He was spirited, vital, and vibrant. All the synonyms.

I'm thinking, *fuck sadness.* Fuck ambivalence. Fuck the unfillable holes. Fuck the compassion play that I call my job, my calling. I'm so weary of it. I'm so bad at it. I can learn. I can grow. From now on, I'll be two steps ahead of the game. I am rage. I am the American electorate, and I'm sick of the establishment, sick of the losses, the endless column of losses.

I'm on Mrs. Fitch's fieldstone patio, entering her toolshed, when my phone rings. Linda.

"How are you holding up, honey?"

"That's ex-honey to you."

"Oh." I hear the worst of a hundred fights in her single syllable, imagine her head tilting down as if to find a spot on her blouse. I taste a hint of remorse, and *I like it*, swishing it around like some new elixir. Like gasoline for my tank.

"How's Randy?" I ask.

"That's not his name."

"Maybe I know him better than you do. Did he tell you about–?"

"That's not why I called."

"The thing with the belt."

"What has gotten into you?"

"The thing with the jumper cables."

"I'm going to hang up now."

"Me, first." Mine's a flip phone. I un-flip it.

Soon, I'm back with two spades and a hand truck inside a wheelbarrow. And a glass dish of potatoes without cheese. Look what happens when you have the kidney to say what you want! And don't want!

"This could be a mistake," Sally says. She's with Boris on the sofa, flipping through the pages of a photo album but not paying attention to the pictures.

"It could be," I say.

"I mean," she says, "how could it not be, Lloyd?"

I don't have an answer, only a sensation. I feel like an eight-year-old boy, naked and tearing through the woods. "Where's Dad?"

I hear the toilet flush upstairs.

"There," I say, leaning over her and pointing. It's a picture of the four of us at the old Gwynn Oak Amusement Park, just down the street from home, circa 1975. "Remember that?"

Now, it's a Park & Ride with a few benches, trees, and a man-made hillock. It's an ashtray, really. A repository for broken glass, condoms, and the neon-red and blue bags from a popular brand of spicy corn chips, but forty years ago, it was the place to be in West Baltimore. There's Dad with baby Sally on his shoulders. His arm is around Mom; they're all squinting. There's me standing in front beneath the bright cast of the sun, staring wide-eyed back at the snapper. I was six-years old and so sure of myself. A wooden roller-coaster, the Mighty Mouse, rises behind us in all its paint-flaking glory. I was an inch shy of almost tall enough, and the man with tattoos on his forehead, took my ticket and Dad's, and said to me, "You'll remember this day, son." And I did…until I forgot.

"I can't remember that far back," Sally says, "but Dad said he'll never forget that ride he took with you."

"Really? He said that?"

"You chucked your corn dog into his lap."

Sound of chairlift descending. Dad has combed Vitalis into his hair. He has changed back into his black suit, white shirt, and red and blue striped tie. His mourning outfit. "Ready?"

"For what?" says Sally. "I'm really confused."

"It's not that fucking complicated," he says.

"What's not? What *is* it?"

"We're going to put your stepmother in her proper hole. The one I paid for. Under the fucking Japanese split leaf maple. Those fuckers."

"Are you kidding," Sally says. "Dig her up?"

He stands on his numbed feet and wills his eighty-three-year old self up like a punch drunk falling back into a fistfight, grabbing at the grail of a knob. "I'm not kidding," he says. "Hand me my quad cane. And that thing too." He points to the portable cd player.

Sally looks at me for help. In her eyes, I see a panic. And good sense maybe. But I'm all in with Dad now. Except, jeez… That's a lot of digging.

"Have you both gone crazy?" Sally asks. "I'm at a loss for words. I can't even think of one fucking word."

I load the shovels and other materials into the back of her truck. We drive in pulsing silence to the Woodlawn cemetery. There's a pond, the ducks, the geese, the mausoleums, and finally the stones.

When Mom died, Dad didn't get angry, not that I can remember. He didn't date. He didn't laugh. He didn't golf. He woke up early and made us our school lunches. Bologna sandwiches in brown paper bags. He made the same for himself. He put his head and shoulders down, and he pushed a mountain of paper until his knees hurt. He did his time, as they say. After a quarter century of good behavior, enter Dot Zicker, a classmate, a companion, and a wife.

When we pull to a stop in front of her grave, Sally finds the word she's been searching for. "Felony."

"There's a higher law," Dad says.

"I hope you have a higher lawyer."

"You don't have to be part of this."

"You can be part of the establishment," I say.

"What?!" she says. "What the fuck does that mean, Lloyd?" She pounds her fist on the hood of the pickup. "I am part of this. I drove, didn't I? I'm here, aren't I? What will you two do if I drive home?"

The first two questions I took to be rhetorical and not so difficult but the third? Even if I can get through all this dirt myself, there's the box, which I can't lift alone and can't move without the truck.

"Will you hand me that?" Dad points to the cd player.

She shakes her head and does as asked.

"We need you, Sweetheart," he says.

The sun is a flaming red disc on the horizon. Within an hour, the sky will be black as my Dad's suit. I turn a slow three sixty, scanning the grounds. I don't see any workers, security, or anyone at all.

"Will you toss me one of those shovels?" I ask Sally.

"Get it yourself," she says, but as I step closer, she throws one at my feet.

I sink the spade into the soft earth. Dad clicks on the music at full volume, Pavarotti sings "Puccini." He sets one of his shiny leather shoes on Dorothy's footstone and appraises the scene.

Look at him. Magnificent. He's on fire. That man!

Figure Eight

"What does *advanced* mean?" Ellie asks.

She and her mother are inching along on a commercial stretch of Highway 116 on the way to the mall. The year is 1994. It's a northern California Christmas Eve morning. Light rain comes with sudden bursts of blinding sunlight.

"Advanced?" asks Donna.

"Daddy said you're advanced."

"It means he wants something."

Ellie shapes her hands like goggles and looks through them at her mother. "But what does *advanced* mean?"

"Like he would know."

"Like I could get an actual answer from you." Ellie sighs. "Like ever."

Donna's brow furrows in the way that means she must now concentrate on driving, must now concentrate on her book, must now concentrate on dinner… It's a face that tells Ellie she's upset, and she'll likely become quiet. As they turn into the crowded mall parking lot, Donna finally says, "Why don't you ask him?"

Ellie draws a triangle through the vapor on her window. "Because…"

"Your father means I've been around." Donna sighs. "He believes in past lives."

"Do you believe in past lives?"

Again, briefly, the brow knits, but this time, it's as if Donna is straining to read a map that only she can see. "I guess I did once. That seems like another life." She laughs. "Listen," she says as they step out of the car. "Oh, never mind. Watch the puddles."

They enter through Macy's, by men's casuals, and are caught in a flurry of shoppers, almost all women shopping for their men. Ellie used to help Donna pick out clothing for her father. *How would Daddy look in a suit with a tie?* It was hard to picture. It was fun. That was only a year ago, but now it seems so much longer.

Ellie finds herself in a men's clothing store on Christmas Eve. She's admiring a display of wool scarves. Garrett, her new leading man, prefers plaid, but she chooses the cornflower blue, because it matches his eyes.

Donna zips through the departments with her hair tucked behind her ears and handbag squeezed beneath her elbow. She has her I-mean-business face on.

Ellie skips every few steps to keep up. "Where are we going to meet Daddy?"

"By the big tree," says Donna.

"What are you going to do?"

"I have to speak with Santa." Donna pauses. "Oh, I forgot. You're done with Santa. You're almost ten now, aren't you?"

Donna and Ellie weave through the last set of Macy's display counters to the main thoroughfare. Gray and white marble tiles slick with the residue of a thousand wet shoes. The air rings tin Christmas jingles. It smells like burnt caramel corn. In front of Kay-Bee Toys, a waist-high electric Santa blows a steady stream of bubbles, and Ellie sees a dark-skinned woman squat to wipe soap off the floor with a rag.

In front of JCPenney, a boy about Ellie's height is talking on a cell phone. The crotch of his pants hangs inches below his knees. After she passes, Ellie looks over her shoulder and sees him examining her mother's backside. She nearly walks into an old man in an electric cart. The man has a clear plastic tube feeding into his nose and a hunted expression on his withered face. "Christmas seems kind of weird this year," she says.

"I don't see your father."

"Are you sure he meant this tree?"

"I don't know what he meant."

"Because there's another tree."

"Of course, there is." Donna sits on a bench and crosses her legs. She curls her shoulders in tight, gives a quick glance back in the direction from which they came, and then fixes her eyes on the tree straight ahead. It's not a tree at all, but a pyramid of potted flowers. Ellie tries to remember if the other tree is an actual tree.

On a square plot of red and silver tinsel grass, felt-covered bears, deer, and penguins wag their heads slowly left and right as their inner wheels turn clockwise and counterclockwise. Ellie had seen inside one once. The head had come off.

She has a sudden sinking feeling, and she tries to imagine what that would look like inside her. She has seen pictures of a human heart, but now she's seeing it mixed with cogs, screws, and blood. But that's way too gross to think about. Instead, she looks to the far end of the wide corridor, near the entrance to Sears, and tries to picture her father walking her way, becoming more himself with each bouncing step. He'd be wearing his jeans and boots. He'd have a heavy key chain attached to his belt. Last week, he wore his purple hooded sweatshirt and a shiny black jacket with Raiders in silver letters on the back.

"I'll give him fifteen minutes," Donna says.

"Then what?"

"We'll see."

The words remind Ellie of Mr. Crispin, the school psychologist. *We'll see* is his favorite expression. "Let's have her go through a few tests," he said, "then we'll see what we know.

It's not often that we have a child who can read at the top of her class in third grade but then falls to the bottom the following year. We'll see."

Ellie and Donna sit on a bench and watch shoppers in silence for what could be fifteen minutes. Donna looks at her watch. Ellie is doubtful but not ready to give up. She pinches and smooths the fabric of her jeans. "We were going to see the movie about the whale or the bear cub."

"I thought you did that last week."

"His car died or something."

"Or something." Donna shakes her head. "So, what did you do?"

"I played with Madame Blab and drew some pictures."

"What did he do?"

Ellie could remember her father lifting a black battery out of the front end of his car and putting a new yellow battery in. He lit incense, beat on a drum, and chanted like a Native American. He said the yellow battery didn't have any juice either. He cooked eggs with cheese. He talked on the phone. She must be careful what she tells her mother about her visits with her father though, especially the last visit. "He put my picture on the refrigerator," she says.

Donna shakes her head again. Whatever Terry does or says, she shakes her head. Since the day Ellie shattered a trophy case at school – what has been referred to as her nervous breakdown – it seems that she and her mother have entered into a kind of bargain, but it was never spoken. Ellie tries not to sulk or have tantrums, and Donna tries not to say bad things about her father. Maybe she has just run out of bad things to say. Irresponsible. Impulsive. Flake. Featherbrain. At least Donna's not screaming or crying any more. She sleeps at night.

Ellie sees a man in a Raiders jacket, but he is much larger than her father. She counts men with moustaches, men with earrings, now sweaters with reindeer, now baby strollers. "Can't we check the other tree?"

Donna shakes her head. "It has been twenty-five minutes, honey."

She feels tears coming and turns her face away from her mother.

"We *can* check the other tree," Donna says softly. "Do you really want to?"

Ellie shakes her head. She touches her eyes with the sleeve of her sweater.

Donna asks, "Want to go shopping with me?"

A woman on an adjacent bench lifts her baby to her breast. The baby's head looks gray to Ellie, or is it just the lights?

She shrugs.

"I have an idea," Donna says. "I think it'll be fun."

"What?"

"A surprise. You'll see." She puts her arm around Ellie's shoulder and combs a lock of Ellie's hair with her fingers. As they make their way back through Macy's, Ellie wonders if her mother *could be* advanced, like someone who has lived life before and knows what to expect. Like maybe she knew it would have been worse to check the other tree and not find him there.

Ellie sits at a bar with her purse and shopping bag holding the seat beside her. She wants to wait for Garrett, but the second time the bartender asks, she says, "Sure. I'll have a Cosmo," and "Is that the right time?" She points to a digital clock behind the bar.

"It's ten minutes fast," the bartender tells her. "Bar time."

Ellie sighs with relief...

Saturday, a week ago, her father, Terry, was scrubbing with the special orange soap he keeps in a tube by the sink. "Hey," he said. "Seems like we weren't meant to see this movie."

"Why don't you get a new car?" Ellie asked.

Terry laughed. "With what money?"

"Maybe Mommy could help you."

"Maybe I'll win the Super Lotto."

"I have almost a hundred dollars."

"You're an angel."

"If I were a real angel, I'd fix your car."

He nodded.

"And I'd make you and Mommy in love again."

He was drying his hands, so he hugged her head between his forearms and his sweatshirt. "If anybody could do it, I'm sure it'd be you." The phone rang. "Whoa. That's Randy. I need to talk to him."

Ellie started her drawing with the face of Madame Blab – her nickname for Madame Blavatsky, Terry's Siamese cat. A friend in school had shown her how to do cats' faces. A square for the nose, with a line descending into a triangle. From the triangle, draw six lines, three on each side for whiskers. Two more triangles for the ears. The eyes were shaped like footballs, and Ellie liked to draw hearts inside them, which Donna had called her trademark.

Of course, she drew a rainbow, a sun in the upper left, and crescent moon in the upper right. She put a fluffy cloud under the rainbow, three butterflies, and a flock of birds like she had seen them done before, like cursive M's. Donna had shown her a trick to give what she called 'an illusion of depth.' She tried obscuring parts of her birds behind the cloud. But the birds didn't look like birds, and the cloud didn't look like a cloud.

"What's that?" Terry asked in passing. "A big spider?"

"Can I have more paper?" Ellie asked.

"Paper doesn't grow on trees," Terry said. "Or does it?" He laughed. "Why don't you fill that one up? Put some people in there. What's a picture without people in it?"

Before Ellie could protest, he was in the bedroom with the door closed. She had some difficult choices. She didn't want to put anyone under the thing that looked like a big swollen spider, so she put Donna in the half-inch space between the margin and the left base of her rainbow. She couldn't leave Terry out, so she put him in the similar space on the opposite side of the page. Now where would she put herself?

She decided to go search for Madame Blab, to look closely and see if the cat's face resembled the face that she had drawn. She opened Terry's bedroom door and walked in on a conversation.

"Yes," Terry said into his phone. "Yes, I know." He was facing the wall and didn't see her. "But Donna can be a mega-bitch."

She closed the door and heard him pleading.

When Terry came out, he rubbed his hands, grinning. "Looks like we got us a ship, Matey," he said in his pirate voice. "The sharks won't get us this time."

"Do you mean Mommy?"

"I mean the scupper hoses," he growled, but when he looked for a smile from Ellie, his face changed. "You know I'm playing, right?"

Ten minutes later in Randy's pickup, Terry said, "Don't tell your mom, but I'm going on a trip, sweetie. I don't know exactly when I'll get back."

Ellie sat in the middle. Randy was driving. His hairy knuckles wrapped tight on the steering wheel. Randy leaned forward and made a face at Terry that Ellie understood to mean, *shut up*.

After a few speed bumps and squeaks from the old springs, Terry said, "It's about money. That's all. Money so I can get my car fixed, and we can have fun together. Money so I can get you a for real Christmas present."

Randy's voice lowered to a strained whisper, "Don't man."

Terry squeezed Ellie's hand on the seat beside him, and he looked at her face until it seemed he couldn't anymore. So, he looked out the window and said, "Don't tell your mom anything. She's got more important things to worry about." His voice sounded apologetic as it often did at the end of a visit. "Donna is advanced, you know. She was a queen in her past life."

Garrett surprises Ellie at the bar. He puts his hands on her shoulders and buries his cold, wet, handsome face in her neck. "So sorry," he says breathlessly. "Rehearsal went long."

"It's nasty out there. So cold and wet," she says. She rubs his hands. "I hope you don't mind that I started without you."

He puts on a pouty face. "How could you?" He's an actor. So, he fakes it well.

Ellie is taken aback for a moment until Garrett kisses her again – a proper kiss, the way Garrett kisses.

To the bartender, he says, "I'll have the same." To Ellie, he says, "You look so far away. Are you all right? You're nervous about meeting my friends? You'll love them. Trust me."

Almost four weeks ago, shortly after Thanksgiving break, Mr. Crispin asked Donna, "You say she's not sleeping well?" He put the same question to Ellie. It was Ellie's first visit into his office since the tests' results came in. Donna had left work early, so she could be there.

"No signs of dyslexia then," Donna said. "I guess that's good news."

"We'll see," Mr. Crispin said. He turned to Ellie, "Are you having nightmares?"

"Not really."

"What about appetite?"

"She pushes her food around the plate," Donna said.

"I like fish sticks," Ellie added. "With ketchup."

"That's true. She eats fish sticks."

"But only with ketchup."

"You don't like any vegetables?"

"Not really," Ellie said.

"Fish sticks was the one dinner her father knew how to make," Donna said.

"I see," Mr. Crispin said. "Is he not around anymore?"

"It has been almost a year," Donna said. "She sees him on Saturdays. Didn't she tell you that?"

Ellie reached for a marble figurine on Mr. Crispin's desk, but she pulled her hand back before touching it.

"That's Claudia," Mr. Crispin said. "See her wings? She can fly."

"No, she can't," Ellie said. "She's just made of whatever."

"She can't without your help." Mr. Crispin smiled. "Pick her up."

Ellie obliged, but she didn't let Claudia soar through the air. Some time, she might like to float Claudia over to the yellow flower on the windowsill, to examine her wings in the light of the sky, but not while her mother is here.

"I'm surprised you didn't tell me about your father," Mr. Crispin said. The tone of his voice was soft and kind, but the remark felt like an accusation.

She wanted to say that it wasn't her fault, but she thought that would be like blaming her mother. She had to drive home with her mother.

Donna said, "Her father and I had some real differences."

"Maybe it's better if I hear it from Ellie."

Ellie said, "I want to go now."

It was a long, uncomfortable silence before Mr. Crispin asked, "Do you mind if I talk with your mother?"

Ellie backed away from the desk and moved out into the hall where she and Claudia examined trophies in a glass case. Some were silver and some were gold; some had a ball attached to a hand atop of an outstretched arm. Others had a ball attached to their foot.

She couldn't hear Mr. Crispin's voice, but she could hear her mother's all too well. "The man refused to grow up. The more we needed him, the more he retreated into fantasies. Wiccans and Druids, Native American horse dancing, the healing powers of hemp, healing crystals. What the hell was making him so sick? And what's so terrible about Depakote?"

Ellie could make Claudia fly, high as she could reach and low as the floor, arcs and spinning loops. Maybe she could even make her dizzy. She held Claudia at arm's length and spun until she felt tipsy, until she fell onto the floor and watched the hallway spin. The wall, the clock, and the trophy case all revolved around her.

"Of course, she misses him. What little girl doesn't miss her daddy? When he wasn't depressed, he was her playmate..."

She struggled to her feet again and spun faster

"A thirty-year-old child. The whole situation was impossible. The best thing would be if he were out of the..."

Spinning until the words blurred, until Claudia, firm in Ellie's fist, crashed into the glass case. And the next thing she heard after the crash was the sound of her mother's voice, "Oh sweetie! Oh my god!" Blood ran off her fingertips, pooling on the floor.

"How do I find my motivation?" Garrett asks, repeating Ellie's question. "I use my life. My memory. What else do I have?"

Ellie stares at him, because he's so new and delightful to look at. Can this be real?

"Well," he continues, "I see you don't believe me. Sometimes, I use my imagination. You know, extrapolate a little bit."

Ellie tries her best to listen, but her thoughts interfere. She wants to reach into her bag and put the new scarf around his neck, admire the blue of it.

"You could do it," Garrett adds.

"Do what?" Ellie asks.

"Let's try," he says. "Show me happy, ecstatic... Your life is a picnic."

Ellie skips around to the passenger door. As she waits for her mother to unlock the doors, she notices the light rain still coming down onto the mall parking lot and the still bright sky in the direction of the highway. There ought to be a rainbow somewhere.

"What was it like being a queen?" Ellie asks.

"Oh god," Donna says. "Did he tell you that? Did he really say that?"

"Were you married to a king? Did you have servants?"

"I don't know, Ellie. That was such a long time ago."

"Did you have a daughter? Was she a princess?"

"You're my only princess," Donna says.

"Come on, Mom."

"Come on, yourself. Look, you got your school shoes soaking wet."

Ellie thinks of the unusual toy on Mr. Crispin's desk. It has six shiny silver balls attached to nylon strings. If you lift one ball and let it drop against the others, another will swing up on the opposite side. If you lift two, two will swing up on the opposite side. It's fun to watch, and it makes a pleasant click-clacking sound. She has amused herself thinking that maybe this is what it's like inside Mommy's head. *Click and clack. Nice and mean. Click and clack. Nice and mean.*

Daddy gets silly and then apologizes. Mommy gets angry and then apologizes. It is something she can always count on.

"You're good at this!" Garrett says, and she is. She's very good at this. Besides, it is easy to imagine feeling happy when what you feel is happy. "Now," Garrett says, "show me sad, bewildered. Life is..."

"Sometimes I like surprises, and sometimes I don't," Ellie says. They're on the highway headed south under an ambivalent sky. It feels good to be out of the mall parking lot and the stop-and-go traffic of Santa Rosa.

"Do you want me to tell you where we're going?"

"Yes. I mean, no." Ellie wants to suppress the excitement in her voice. She imagines bees flying into a zippered pouch. "I want you to tell me about the other thing."

"About my past life," Donna says, flatly. "I want you to promise that you won't get caught up in this silliness."

"I won't. I just want to know."

"You promise?"

"Yes, Mom."

Donna lets out a long slow breath. "I was about to finish school, and I needed to find a job."

"You met Daddy at school, right?"

"We both worked in the food service, but I needed a *real* job, something to pay off my loans. So, he, your father, brought me this flier that said, *Find out your true calling.*

"Like if you're a queen or not?"

"That's not what I expected! When I saw what was going on, I would've just left if it hadn't been for him. You know how excited he can get – the most gullible man alive."

Ellie realizes that the ache in her hand is from keeping it in a tight fist. She spreads her fingers as wide as she can. "Yeah, I know."

"But *I* never said I was a queen."

"Daddy said that."

"So, first this woman got a whole group of us in a guided meditation. Like a hypnosis."

"Why?"

"To go back."

To go back? Ellie wants to ask more, but she's afraid her mother won't continue.

"What I remember is walking barefoot through a courtyard. I was looking down, because I had a veil on. I had a gold ring on one of my toes. My feet were dark brown, almost black, and the ground was hot and sandy. People were bowing on both sides of me, forming a path. I had to be careful not to step on their hands." The rain slows to a few drops on the glass. Donna cuts off the windshield wipers.

"What else?"

"I remember feeling embarrassed because of all the attention. It felt like heat on my face." She has that concentrated look again, but Ellie can see a hint of a smile too. "Oh, there was music. Some kind of deep sounding horn and drums. Two maidens, dark and pretty, lifted my veil."

"What did you see?"

"Stairs. A long flight of stairs."

"And then?"

"I only remember what I felt -- safe and cared for. There was something I had to do, but I didn't know what."

"You probably had to go sit on your throne."

"I probably had to get a real job," Donna says. She pulls into the right lane and slows the car down a bit. They must be getting near to where they're going.

"And then?"

"That's it."

"That's it? That's no big deal at all!"

"I'm glad you think so. The way your father carried on..."

"I mean, it's like boring."

"All right, all right." Donna laughs. "You don't have to be rude about it."

"Say you're my leading lady," Garrett says. He sips from his Cosmo and turns his blue eyes on her.

She giggles. "I like to say that."

"Let's say, I'm missing. Maybe I've been killed at war or something. It doesn't matter why. It's only make-believe of course, but the emotion is real. You have to call up the emotion. Remember. Imagine. Give it a try."

Last Christmas Eve, Randy had come to visit. Randy's ponytail lay flat against his back, but Daddy was wearing his high, so it stuck out like a pony's. Mommy was baking cookies and sipping from a bottle of beer. Randy and Daddy sat at the kitchen table talking. Sometimes they sucked smoke through a long plastic tube. The smells were complicated like a burning field but also sweet like vanilla.

Daddy talked fast as usual but in a low voice. His hands were dancing, and Mommy looked annoyed like she often did. He said that he was going to write a book that would make *us* rich. He called it *How to Be Stupid for Idiots*. Ellie had wanted to know what was so funny, but no one would answer her question since they were all laughing, even Mommy.

She remembers a hike in the Colonel Armstrong Redwoods Reserve. The time, she twisted her ankle, and Daddy lifted her onto his shoulders.

"Don't," Mommy warned. "You'll hurt your back."

But Daddy did it anyway, and from her perch, she could see the top of Mommy's head, the part in her hair, and even where the individual hairs came out of her scalp. Mommy came close and kissed her on the knee before kissing Daddy on the mouth. It made a wet sound like when you break a celery stick. That was the summer more than a year ago.

She remembers Daddy explaining why he bought a telescope – that he had read a poem about stars. Something about the difference between stars and clouds. Things that last and things that don't. She didn't remember his words so well as his look when Mommy said, "But you don't have a job. The wood under the deck needs to be replaced, and what about your car? What about the phone bill?" The smile froze on his face, but his eyes flashed like a light bulb just before it dies.

She remembers the night that she sat on her bed, playing with her Polly Pockets. Mommy and Daddy had been arguing, but then it got quiet.

She heard Mommy say, "Take this too."

But he said, "No, I got it for Ellie."

"The hell you did."

Ellie never knew for sure what *it* was, but she never saw the telescope again.

She remembers the time the three of them went to the beach, and she had wandered around some rocks and onto another beach. She thought, *I should let them know where I am, or I'll be in trouble.* She saw more anemones than she had ever seen, so many that it seemed as if the rocks were alive. She counted five starfish. It was exciting and scary like she had stumbled onto another planet. She thought: *They'll come and find me. They always find me.*

It's not as if there's any pattern to it. Old memories and newer memories. Happy and sad memories pop up often, almost always when she's trying to read. Mr. Crispin, Ms. Bell, her teacher, and Mommy talk about the importance of concentration, but how does that work? It's like building brick walls inside your mind. Like keeping things out. Like pushing things away.

She tries not to think scary thoughts when she's alone in bed. Don't think about the man with the eye patch who offers to work in the yard. Don't think about the movie with bugs crawling up out of the toilet. But what about these other thoughts that always leave you staring out windows and little holes in cinder block walls.

Ellie tries, briefly and halfheartedly. She tries to change the subject, but Garrett is too excited, determined. "Is this what you actors do for fun?" she asks. "I'm not sure this is my *idea of fun."*

"Please," he says. "Try this once for me. You've lost something or someone, and it hurts and…"

"I'm kind of glad we got out of that mall," Ellie says.

"Oh, me too!" Donna pulls up on the emergency brake and gives Ellie a pat on the knee. "I don't think you'll remember this place. It has been so long."

Ellie doesn't recognize the building: brown and pink stone facade, squarish. She sees red, electric letters, barely illuminated against the overcast sky: CAL - SKATE. Only two other cars are in the lot.

"Hey," Donna says, "there might not be much under the tree tomorrow, you know? I was hoping that today I–"

"You mean Santa."

"Yeah, whatever," Donna says. "Anyway, I'm sorry if Christmas–"

"It's okay." Ellie manages a thin smile. She had wanted more Polly Pockets for her collection and a bell for her bike, and there was something else. But she can't say it.

"Gosh," Donna says, "you must have been four when we came here last."

"Did Daddy come with us?" She wants to say, *Daddy went on a trip to get money.* She wants to say that he's going to get his car fixed and something special for her, but he made her promise not to tell. Donna might not believe it anyway. She's not sure she believes it all either, so she wants to say it out loud as if that will make it real. Instead, she swallows a big gulp of air that spreads like a hole in her chest.

"I guess he was with us," Donna says, letting out her breath. Like the click-clacking balls, she bounces back to her nice, happy voice. "I never told you that I love to skate. I used to be pretty good. Skating got me through a rough patch when I was about your age."

She tries again, for Garrett. She doesn't want to imagine that he has gone missing or has been killed. It is hard enough to believe that he is here with her, that this is real. But she does not want him to think of her as a coward. She tries to call up some of her sad memories...

Ellie and Donna pass through the heavy glass doors into the foyer. On the far wall, Ellie sees a cotton banner, green field, red letters: WE LOVE YOU, BOBBY. A girl in a burgundy-colored vintage dress sits on the floor with her back against the wall. As they get closer, Ellie sees that the girl's eyebrow is pierced, a small silver cross reflects the dim light. Leaning in the next doorway is a boy in a navy-blue windbreaker and a black necktie knotted like a child's fist. He looks as if he had made a special effort to comb his wild hair, like maybe he had never tried before. They look as if they may be in the middle of an argument, but no one is speaking.

Neither the boy nor the girl shows any acknowledgment of Ellie and Donna until Donna asks, "Is there skating here today?"

The girl tilts her head in the direction of the open doors.

Donna walks to the counter where shoes are exchanged for roller skates. There is a light in the back, and there appears to be someone moving among the wire racks stuffed with boxes.

Ellie pauses before a glass case. Inside is a bulletin board pinned with roughly fifty snapshots. It doesn't take long for her to realize the same boy is in every picture. In some, he appears to be about sixteen. He has soft features and an unusually sweet, earnest smile.

"Hello," Donna calls back into the shadows.

"Mom, look," says Ellie. "That's the swimming hole near our house. That's the rope swing."

"Is Bobby on the swing," says the girl in the other room. Her accent is a surprise like one of the twin girls on the TV show that Ellie likes. The one who lives in Paris and has nice dresses. "Bobby always so careful."

"Shit. He stood on that rock for twenty minutes," the boy says. "And he still didn't even swing."

"That what really sucks," the girl says. "Should be one of us. Not him."

"Didn't have nothing to do with being careful."

"Shut up."

"You think everything happens for a reason. Some shit just happens."

The girl punches the carpet. "Please, shut up!"

Ellie tries to turn her attention back to the photos. They had seemed like such happy pictures, but now they all are tainted, strange.

"Anyway," the girl says, composed. "Is cool on the river. What you doing way down here?"

"Skating, I guess," Ellie says.

Donna strides up to Ellie's side with a puzzled expression. She examines the photos behind the glass.

"It's kind of a private party," the boy says.

"I wouldn't call it party," the girl counters. "Memorial."

"Yeah. Another memorial."

"Shut up."

"Nobody has showed up." The boy shrugs. "You can probably skate."

"Just ask Mrs. Breughel," the girl says.

"That's Bobby's mom," says the boy.

"I don't know," Donna says. "I mean, we didn't even know him."

Ellie is startled by the sudden presence of a woman standing beside her mother. She seems unusually tall and disproportionate until Ellie sees that she is on skates. *Why is this spooky?* The woman's eyes are thick with tears, yet she is smiling. "Of course, you can skate," she says. "Bobby loves to skate." Her voice is slow and breathy, almost sleepy.

Ellie searches the other faces to see if this is for real, but everyone except the woman seems uncomfortable, hiding their eyes.

The girl finally speaks up. "Bobby was good skater."

"Yeah," the boy agreed.

"His friends will be here soon," the woman says.

The boy turns abruptly to look at the girl. The girl tilts her head down toward the carpet. Ellie knows the look. It means *ssshhh.* It means, *just let it go.* It's like Randy telling Daddy to cool it or like the many bedtimes when Donna had been reading and Ellie had cut in with "When is Daddy coming back?"

"*Ssshhh* now," her mother would say, or she'd appear to study the fabric of the bedspread.

Mrs. Breughel skates slowly, awkwardly, about twenty feet to a metal box on the wall beside the concession stand. She flips switches until a mirror ball starts spinning and floodlights shine. The rink itself almost appears to be spinning with the revolving flecks of red, and green and white. "Now, it's beginning to feel like Christmas," she says.

"Well?" Donna asks.

Ellie shrugs.

"Come on," Donna says. "I guess we'll need some skates," she tells Mrs. Breughel.

Mrs. Breughel pushes herself across the carpet from chair to chair to wall. She looks as if she'll break if she falls. A minute later, she appears at the opposite side of the counter. "What sizes?"

"Three for her and an eight and a half for me."

When Mrs. Breughel sets the two pair on the counter she says, "You've got a beautiful little girl."

"I know it," Donna says. She smiles at Ellie.

"You're special." Mrs. Breughel reaches across the counter and brushes the backs of her cold fingers against Ellie's cheek.

Ellie recoils slightly, looking at her mother.

"You love to skate," Mrs. Breughel says.

"I don't know how," Ellie says.

"Nonsense."

"She doesn't remember the last time we came," Donna says. "It has been so long."

"Nonsense," Mrs. Breughel says again. Ellie can't help but look at the woman's face. She is pretty or was once, but something isn't right about her. Perhaps it is the deep set of her eyes that reminds Ellie of a mask.

Garrett pulls his bar stool an inch closer and squeezes her hands. He whispers words of encouragement.

"Skating, you never forget," says Mrs. Breughel.

Donna leans on the counter. "I'm sorry about your son."

Mrs. Breughel stiffens, pulling back. "There's no need to be sorry. His friends will be here soon. Bobby wouldn't miss a chance to be with his friends."

Ellie and Donna take their skates to a bench beside the rink. As Donna is tightening the laces for Ellie, she whispers, "Poor woman. So sad."

Ellie sits quietly and waits while her mother laces her own pair. Her eyes settle on the mirror ball, but her mind is working fast. *What a weird day it has been, and it just keeps getting weirder.*

"Are you ready?" Donna asks.

"No."

"Are you okay?"

"I don't know."

"I think that woman upset you."

"How do you go back? I mean…" She pauses, because upon saying the words out loud, she understands that this is exactly what she has been meaning to ask. It's what she needs to know. *How do you make Christmas like Christmas? How do you get your concentration back? How do you go back to feeling safe?* "How do you go back to another life?"

"Oh Ellie," Donna groans.

"Please Mom."

"Please what?"

"How?"

"I don't want to have that conversation. If you must, you can talk to your father about that."

"No, I can't," Ellie says. "I can't." Tears and mucous flow out. The feeling she has been suppressing all day, all week, and for most of a year, bursts forth, and she can't stop her chest from rising and falling, can't settle her breathing, can't slow the bloody cogs, and can't hold it in, shove it away, or fight it one second longer. "But– Mom," she says through her paroxysm. "It's all I'm asking…" Breathless, melodramatic sobs. "It-could-be-my-Christ-mas-pres-ent."

Donna sits for a moment in silence, hands helplessly in her lap before she stands. She rolls several feet to the rink's entrance, rolls back, and leans over the banister. Her face is just inches from Ellie's. "Watch," she says. "I hope I can still do this."

Ellie remembers her last visit with Terry at a group home in Cotati, where every two weeks, she brings him a carton of cigarettes and sits with him on a well-worn sofa in the common room. She hears about his secret soulmate in Sedona – The Timeless One – again and it makes her sad, particularly the sight of him waiting in line to get his dose at the office door.

She remembers the last time she saw her mother, Donna. She was folding laundry in her house and talking about getting away together, just the two of them. Maybe to Mount Shasta or Lake Tahoe. She loves the snow, the softness of, the roundness…

But twenty-two years later, Ellie is still Ellie and her mind, as always, has a mind of its own. It takes her back to a Christmas Eve at a skating rink with her mother.

Ellie lowers her head. Now, when she needs her nice mommy most of all, she gets the mean one. Or maybe not. She can't be sure. Hesitantly, she looks behind her to see if anyone else has witnessed her tantrum, and she sees the face of Mrs. Breughel, eyes still shimmering, trance-like, with that expectant smile. She can't bear to look at her.

She sees the French girl and the boy, both now standing in the doorway, looking toward her mother.

In spite of herself, Ellie turns to face the rink. She watches through a blur of tears. With the spinning flecks of colored light, it seems almost unreal.

"...like the movie of a dream," she says.

"What?" Garrett shakes his head. "I don't understand. Now you're smiling?" Again, he affects the tone of indignation. "You've lost your leading man and --"

" Ssshhh" Ellie says.

Her mother pushes off and executes a graceful spin. Her hands are folded behind her back, and the breeze of her motion presses her bangs tight against her forehead. She skates half a revolution around the oval rink, pirouettes, and then returns in a flawless backwards figure eight.

Donna leans over the banister again. "As soon as you're ready, I'll teach you how to do that. That will be your Christmas present from me."

Proximity

The first time I lost Lucy was at the Women's March in D.C., 2017. She was three years old, forty pounds, and I carried her on my shoulders until she squirmed and the ache in my neck became a pounding in my head. The moment I set her on the ground, a push from behind sent me into the back of a coworker from my hometown in northern California.

"Kate! What a surprise!" Marta said, beaming at me with tears in her eyes. She threw her arms around me. "Meet my husband, Jim." He threw his arms around me too. I barely knew her, and I'd never seen him before. Such a sudden show of affection tends to make my blood shy. So do marches and rallies in fact. I have a low tolerance for public expression of emotion – be it of love or rage – both of which had been maximally on display for hours.

What was I doing there, so far from home?

As Marta reached into her bag to give me a pin and pink hat, I turned to look for Lucy. Her pigtails, tied in pink ribbons, were lost in a sea of crotches.

Thus, began the most terrifying fifteen minutes of my life.

She couldn't have been more than twenty feet away, but which direction did she go in? I couldn't move. I couldn't stand still. I made my search in ever widening concentric circles, pushing at times against the forward thrust of the crowd. Lucky for me, Lucy chose to sit cross-legged on the pavement. Lucky for both of us she wasn't trampled.

Fast forward two and a half years to the May Day March in Santa Rosa, a Wednesday midafternoon. Lucy is almost six now. Marta is still my coworker, a lawyer at the Immigrants' Legal Defense Center, and I am still a paralegal. I am also still separated from my own partner, who is also a Jim. I am still a single mother. What's different in this case is that Marta and several other lawyers from the ILDC have planned an act of civil disobedience, and I've agreed, somewhat reluctantly, to be the contact person. My job is to collect cell phones, purses, and information lest any of my fellow workers be carted off to jail.

Also, it's worth noting, Lucy had and has and always will have Down Syndrome. The thumb of one hand is often lodged deep in her mouth. With the other, she tends to tug at the waist of her T-shirt. Like many children her age, she is easily disoriented in crowds, but strangers, well-intended or not, tend not to look at her or to briefly look and turn away. She is indiscriminately affectionate, and it seems for now to assume that others feel what she feels.

What does she feel? Every day is her birthday. Every sunrise promises cake and ice cream, songs and surprises. She feels loved, because it is all she knows, and it is all I ever want her to know. She has refused to wear a harness, and I don't blame her. She permitted me to tie the string of a blue helium balloon around her wrist.

I've always had trouble finding a babysitter, so in the weeks before the march and action, I did not attend the CD training nor any of the planning meetings. I was fuzzy on the details. We'd meet on Sebastopol Road, walk roughly a mile with the full procession to downtown Santa Rosa. Most would gather in the plaza in front of the mall, but our small contingent would cross the street and protest in front of Wells Fargo, effectively blocking the entrance and exit from the B Street side of the bank. Wells Fargo is heavily invested in the private, for-profit prisons, which hold immigrants and asylum seekers detained by ICE or agents of the Border Patrol.

What you've heard is true. They separate families. They hold children in cages. I've seen the pictures. I've heard the wailing of toddlers on YouTube. I've met some cousins, uncles, and grandmothers who are miles from the border, grieving and weeping. I can't imagine the pain that the children feel, nor the psychological harm that will come from these abrupt divisions. I think I can imagine what the mothers are going through, but I will not allow myself to dwell on it. I can't.

For now, Lucy has half of one hand in her mouth, and the other is in a fist gripping the back pocket of my jeans. Marta, Celeste, and Rodrigo, who are also lawyers, are several paces ahead in this crowd of roughly five hundred.

An energetic young man with a megaphone is leading the marchers in a chant, "Wells Fargo, you're the worst! Put our immigrant families first!" and "Hey! Hey! Ho! Ho! Detention camps have got to go!" I see a sign that reads 'Justice for Palestinians' and a large banner that says, 'Fight for Fifteen.' A man wears a faded T-shirt with a familiar looking logo: *It's Mueller Time.* One big war, fighting on so many fronts.

When I turn to make sure Lucy isn't drooping, the blue balloon brushes my face. It could be Jim; it's the color of his eyes.

It is a reminder of my internal preoccupations, not that I need one. We were engaged. He was twenty-five; I was thirty-one. We never fought or not so that anyone witnessing would have perceived it. He wasn't ready to have a child but willing to think about it. He had wanted me to abort when we learned Lucy would be born with a disability.

"Why now?" he said. "Why bring more suffering into the world?"

"We'll bring more love into the world," I insisted. I believe wholeheartedly in a woman's right to choose, but I simply could not make the choice he wanted. King Solomon got the last word: *Go on then and pull your relationship apart.*

Fifty feet ahead, a five-piece marching horn section punches up the energy. A dozen men and women in Mayan headdress perform a ritualistic dance even though two are working with Hula Hoops and the two others are on rollerblades.

Lucy tugs. "ABC Mommy." She's referring to our favorite YouTube video, the Jackson Five. It's the only song she knows by name. She waddles when she walks and often rocks when she sits. But when I play "ABC," she rocks full tilt.

I turn, squat, and kiss her on the cheeks. She smiles. She's a trooper for now, and I'm so proud of her that it nearly chokes me. "1, 2, 3. Baby, you and me."

She gives me a wet high five.

Because it is a permitted march, we have the SRPD on motorcycles as escorts. The tail end of the procession hits the beginning of rush hour. Some motorists signal support with a beep of the horn or a pumped fist. Others look on annoyed, and some few flip us the bird.

As we get closer to our destination, Marta and Celeste offer a fuller description of our planned action. Two (names I instantly forget) will go inside the bank with a banner and leaflets, describing the reasons WF should divest. They have a letter that they hope to deliver to the bank manager. If the police ask them to leave, they will leave. It is important not to startle or frighten customers.

As for the other part of the action, a handyman constructed a facsimile of a cage for us, a four by four square of chain-link fence, roughly four feet high. Marta, Celeste, Rodrigo and another whose name I didn't catch will carry the cage across the street from the plaza and set it in front of the bank doors. They will stand inside the cage. I'll stand beside them, outside of the cage. Marta had not anticipated that I'd bring Lucy, and I think she's unhappy about it, but it's too late to make any new arrangements.

Is it possible I'll be swept up by the police, arrested along with the others? I simply can't let that happen. It's terribly unfortunate that Jim is out of town. He would have been here if I had asked him. In spite of our differences and his choice to live apart, Jim has always had my back when I needed him. He had said in the months before Lucy was born that he wasn't sure he could love her, but once she came into the world, there was never any question that he did. And she worships him.

And here I am thinking about Jim, the sad turn in our lives, the desperate hope that he'll change his mind, the subtle signs he might, when I should be helping carry the cage across B Street.

Lucy lets go of my pocket in the middle of the crosswalk. She stops to point at a larger than life puppet with an enormous orange papier-mâché head. Beside the puppet, a man is selling frozen desserts from a cart. Of course, that's where the fun is, but we need to press on.

I take Lucy's hand and pull as she tries to sit in the middle of the road, all seventy-five pounds of her. I am barely strong enough to drag her to the sidewalk in front of the bank. Bikes, cars, and buses whizz by. I bribe her. "You're such a big girl. Happy Meal. Rainbow colored snow cone. And I lie. "Soon. Very soon."

She slumps beside the bank's wall only a few steps from where I must stand.

The cage is in place with the lawyers in the cage. It's loose; it feels good. Lawyers trade lawyer jokes. Soon, the protesters from inside the bank join us on the outside, pulling their ten-foot banner, chanting, "¡Sin justicia, no hay paz!"

Soon, a tall, bald man in a suit pushes the bank doors open a crack and speaks to Marta, Celeste, and Rodrigo. "You need to move," he says. "You're blocking the door."

"We know," says Marta. "We're not going to move."

"I will call the police."

"We're prepared for that," Marta says.

He retreats. A moment later, he's back. "You are creating a fire hazard. You're putting the customers in danger."

"They can exit on the other side of the bank."

"You're making a terrible inconvenience."

"That's the point," Celeste says.

The police arrive as promised. I count two SUVs, ten motorcycles, and roughly a dozen cops on foot. After a lengthy conference at curbside, one emerges as spokesman, approaching the cage. Even though I am close, I cannot hear the exchange, because an energetic young man with the megaphone is standing only a foot away roaring, "Si Se Pueda! ¡Si Se Pueda!"

I feel a headache coming on but also a rush of adrenaline. It's in the air.

Rodrigo calls me closer, telling me that the group has decided to go limp if arrested. His pupils are double-sized, and his voice breathless.

Lucy is still sitting, sucking on her wrist. She seems to be trying to pry off the string, the tether to her blue buoy.

Minutes pass, and Marta beckons me to the edge of the cage. She's an old hand at this. She wants me to know how things are likely to unfold. "Now that the police have dispersed and it is quarter after five, they might simply wait it out. The bank closes at six."

"Oh," I say. "Will you be disappointed?"

She shrugs. "We'll be in the paper tomorrow in any case." She smiles. "It's just the beginning."

Celeste comes to Marta's side and gives her a squeeze. To me, she says, "Thank you. I know it wasn't easy bringing your little girl along for this." She makes a visor with her hand and looks into the crowd. "By the way, where is Lucy?"

I point to the space where she had been sitting. Any parent must know this moment of terror. When I turn, I see the blue balloon blowing across B Street, see the broad side of a bus fill the space between me and her. I hear the screech of horns and the squeal of tires. I feel the weight of wet sandbags in my legs. It takes a lifetime to cross ten feet to the curb.

A man – a total stranger – lifts Lucy off the street. I wave frantically as he carries her toward me. She is unharmed, oblivious.

But I also see the boy who held the megaphone leapt into the onrushing traffic.

Later, I will learn his name. Pedro. He is a student at Santa Rosa Junior College. He is an advocate for day laborers, an amateur accordion player, an undocumented immigrant from Guatemala, a rabid Warriors fan, a collector of tats, a pot smoker, and an embarrassment to his friends on karaoke night. He got a broken leg and a frightening concussion.

He might've died.

He stopped the traffic. He didn't hesitate.

Love and suffering. Suffering and love.

Gather your courage and come back, Jim. Do you see, we've only touched the surface?

AN ORDINARY LOVE STORY

Betty leaves Ryan with her brother and sister-in-law in Santa Rosa. He hasn't napped, but he's fine as soon as they give him hot chocolate in his Sippy Cup and set him down in front of a big flat screen TV. He immediately takes the remote in his four-year old fist, clicks to one of those Third Reich things on the History Channel, and clicks again to a woman with a shapely sweater and a broad smile who's modeling jewelry. Betty exits without saying goodbye to him. No tugging at clothes and no bawling. Thank God.

Next, she drops Cassie, who's going on 13, at a girlfriend's house for an overnight visit. "Don't forget your backpack," Betty says. "Did you put a toothbrush in?"

Cassie looks as if it takes superhuman strength to endure such a question. She shuts the door and leans her tortured, pretty face in the window. "Anything else, Mom?"

"Nothing, honey." She watches as Cassie drags her feet down the gravel drive, pulling her stonewashed jeans over the crest of her fleshy hips, only to have them slide back down. She taps the horn.

The girl turns, beleaguered, and shuffles back to the open window.

"How about the hairbrush?"

"I can't even believe this."

"And Cassie?"

"What?"

"I'm sorry."

"What for?" Cassie asks, then, "Yes, Mom. I heard it already like a dozen times."

She permits Cassie to reach the same low spot in the driveway that she had reached before and taps the horn again. She can't resist.

The girl, it seems, is on the brink of becoming whoever it is she might be, and Betty needs to watch. She knows Cassie will not return to the side of the car, but her head will turn with her brow pinched – such a perfect show of suffering.

With the late afternoon sun lighting up the windshield, Cassie won't see the smile on her mother's lips or the tears brimming in her eyes.

On highway 101 South to Route 12 East toward the E Street group home, she hears Venezuela's president, Hugo Chavez, on the radio. Spanish and English. It's hard to follow. He was talking about U.S. Imperialism in the southern hemisphere. Why is he now talking about poverty in Africa? It seems every conflict leads to another with its own complex history. An endless chain of sticky contingencies. The world is shrinking and expanding at the same time, every toothache is a symptom of heart disease. But she breathes and tells herself that it's not her worry. It can't be right now.

She's on her way to deliver a carton of Camel Lights and a bottle of dandruff shampoo to Karl, to sign the guest book, to be polite and unflappable, and to avoid that tough-love bitch Penny, the Program Manager, at all costs.

"No," she tells Kevin, standing in the office doorway. "There's no alcohol in the shampoo. I checked."

Behind her, in the kitchen, a bald man in a sleeveless T-shirt and with tufts of black hair sprouting from his upper arms, lifts heaping spoons full of toasted oats to his mouth. She watches him until he looks up at her.

"Yes," she tells Kevin. "I know about the 10 Day Freeze." At the last place, they called it *Blackout,* which was a subtle sign of humor, she had hoped, but there was never any supporting evidence of such. It means: no visitors, no phone calls, and no leaving the premises. Karl survived two days in the last program before he went AWOL, but he wasn't court ordered that time. He didn't have jail hanging over his head.

"I'll come see him next week," she tells Kevin. "When he's settled in."

She sees Karl in the yard on her way out. He's on his knees, weeding the garden. He's wearing the khaki shorts that he wore three days ago when she brought him here. They look clean from fifty feet away. He has shaved off his sideburns. He looks like Ryan, and she feels again as if she might suddenly laugh, cry, or both. She walks toward her car quickly.

After she turns the corner past the one-room building called Meetings, she hears his voice. "Betty? Bet?"

If she were to stop, what would she say to him? Would she tell him that she closed her eyes and sniffed his shampoo? That the aroma triggered a pounding pulse in her sternum and a subtle gag reflex? Would she say that she has decided to look out for herself? That she's on her way to a class right now? That if she meets someone nice – a man – and he asks her to coffee, she'll…

She'll probably freak.

Route 12 West to Highway 101 North to Mendocino Avenue and to the Junior College. The radio reports the numbers of casualties in Iraq and Afghanistan, and brief testimonies from the displaced victims of Hurricane Katrina. It wasn't long ago that Betty listened with a strange sense of hope, a belief that when things got bad enough, people would come to their senses. Isn't that how it's supposed to work? Critical mass? One hundred monkeys or something?

She had taken a passing interest in Cindy Sheehan's campaign at Camp Casey. She had signed dozens of Internet petitions and even stood on the corner of River Road and Armstrong Woods with a banner, Karl, and the kids. It was one of the few things she and Karl did together that she felt good about.

But now, even though Betty may be hearing the news, she's not listening. She parks off campus. She should hurry, but she doesn't. She checks the contents of her backpack – a new five-subject spiral bound notebook, a plastic bag of ballpoint pens, and a couple of rubber dinosaur refrigerator magnets that Ryan must have tossed in. The class is called Introduction to Fiction Writing. She could have chosen to take Money Management, which is much more practical, or Local Geology, which promises a coastal outing at the end of semester, but the blurb in the catalog for this class appeals to her more than the others: *supportive and challenging, a place to risk real self-expression.*

The word *risk* is what pulled her in. How long has it been since she was not in damage control mode? When was the last time she tried something new?

She enters the classroom fifteen minutes late and sits in the front row, in the last remaining chair. Everyone is writing, even the teacher, who is seated cross-legged on a table in front of the room with a pad on his lap. Behind him on the board, she reads: Prof. McCauley.

She takes out her notebook and a fresh pen. Her heart sinks. Except for the teacher, the only man in the class appears to be in his mid-seventies. The teacher has red-orange hair, cut close on the sides with curls on top, and wire-rimmed glasses. He looks like he's too young to buy a beer.

Of course, Betty doesn't know what the assignment is, but she writes anyway. She had won an honorable mention in high school for "Second Chances," which was a story loosely based on real events about identical twins, girls.

In the real account, one of the girls had dated an older boy, reportedly a small-time dope dealer. The girl disappeared for two weeks, and the story of her disappearance dominated the nightly news and prompted a thorough police search, including divers in wet suits searching the riverbed near where the girl was last seen. Betty's account, like the news, had focused on the missing girl, the mystery of her disappearance, and the celebration when she was recovered. All those years ago she had chosen to call the girls Remington and Madison and the bad boy's name was Chad, but this time around, she'll make some changes.

He'll be called Spike, for example. The missing girl, Kari, may or may not be found; she's not sure yet. In any case, Betty's interest now is in Amber, the not-so-newsworthy twin. She doesn't know where she'll go with all this – doesn't have a clue – only that she wants a scene, a real showdown, where Amber confronts Spike.

"Stop," says Professor McCauley. "Time's up."

****
****

A small part of the problem is that every name, song, book, film, or joke seems familiar. It's all on the tip of the tongue, hovering above the hazy horizon of consciousness. For most hours of the day, Karl's mind is a waterlogged newspaper.

A part of the problem is that alcohol is clarifying. A few drinks tend to engage that thing that fits into that other thing and makes it turn. Cogs. Cognition. A full bottle can turn random noise into a melody. Now it's as if he hears claws scratching, a rusty wheel grinding.

The Program Manager, Penny, is preceded by the jangle of keys on her belt. "Meetings," she says. "Everyone. Two minutes."

"Which meeting?" the man with hairy arms asks.

"You have a schedule, Marvin," Penny replies. "You can read, can't you?"

After Penny passes, Karl says, "Seemed like a reasonable question. I don't know why she had to bite your head off."

"I don't know," Marvin says, expressionless. Minutes later, he confides to the group. "I think someone here wants to interfere with my program." He looks in Karl's direction and then down into his lap.

"Oh Christ," Karl mumbles.

"Do you have something you want to say?" Penny asks.

"No."

"Because it seemed like–"

"I've been here four days, and I already can't stand it," Karl says. "I don't know how I'm going to last three fucking months."

"Language, please," Lee, Karl's sullen roommate, says.

Penny nods approvingly at Lee.

"One day at a time," Cherise says, who is a Level III and hopes to graduate in a week.

"Let's make it two days at a time," Karl says.

"That'll do," Penny says. "But if you want my opinion, I don't think you'll make it."

"I'll make it," Karl says.

"We'll see."

"What choice do I have?"

****
****

The kids are finally sleeping after an unusually long and difficult bedtime routine. Cassie threw a fit when Betty cut the video about the girl skating champion off.

"Since when did you get so mean?" she asked. "You don't have to take all of your problems out on me!"

Ryan refused to wear the Batman pajama bottoms with the Spiderman top, fifteen extra minutes waiting for the dryer. Now, he holds Betty's hair in his fist, lightly snoring. She peels herself free from him, one sweaty little finger at a time, tiptoes from his bed to the door, and pulls it almost shut behind her. She places a flat bag of popcorn in the microwave and snaps on the TV. It's a rerun. She watches for five minutes, but her mind is elsewhere.

Professor McCauley had said that he doesn't want any fluff. No breezy summer vacation stories. He wants high stakes and emotional truth. She had felt a flush when he said that. She'll show him she's up to the challenge. She has decided that even if he is gay like she thinks he is, she's going to make him fall in love with her. She opens her spiral bound notebook on the kitchen table and begins where she had left off in class:

Amber and Kari had not been close in the months before Kari's disappearance. Few words passed between them; they simply couldn't stand the sight of one another. Oh, perhaps once or twice, Kari had made an effort to explain her mind to Amber, but Amber was frightened, and her fear showed as disdain.

Kari had become a stranger in her own house. To her parents, the reasons added up to one – Spike. "Spike exerted a negative influence on Kari," they said. No, that's not how they said it. They said, "That boy is nothing but bad news."

It was so obvious, even someone who didn't know Kari could see it. Soon after Kari started dating Spike, she stopped doing her homework. Her scores on tests and quizzes had been mediocre but soon dropped through the floor. She did a poor job on her chores and would have ignored them altogether if not for the threat of being grounded. She cut classes. She slipped out of the house at night and slept in late on weekend mornings. Kari, it seemed, didn't care. She had even started wearing black mascara and silver lipstick.

Almost two weeks after Kari's disappearance on a Sunday afternoon, Amber said to her parents, "Let's go out for ice cream." Judging from the look on their faces, she might have said, "I've been impregnated by aliens."

But their faces, like their thoughts, would not hold still for long. She saw her father's gaze return mile by sad mile to his hands on the knees of his trousers. She saw her mother's hard mouth quiver but then soften.

"Okay," her mother said. "Let's."

"I think that's a fine idea," her father agreed.

Ten minutes later from the now enormous backseat of her parents' Volvo Wagon, Amber asked, "What's going to happen to Spike?"

"Please don't mention that name," her father said.

A familiar, sickly silence followed. Amber settled back into the worn upholstery, sighed, and watched the phone wires rising and falling through her window.

"He was being held for possession of marijuana," her mother said quietly. "No other charges can be filed until... Until they find..."

"He has been released on bail," her father said with acid in his voice. "Free to come and go as he pleases."

It's past midnight. Betty turns the pages to the next subject section of her notebook and scribbles:

milk

cat food

sunscreen

C's book report

K's foot powder

Amber has a plan!

****
****

Karl is standing in the office beside Penny's desk. He's required to phone Betty and tell her not to visit on Tuesday between four and six.

"Hello," Betty says.

"Hi," Karl responds. "You can't come this week. I'm still on restriction."

"Why?"

"Were you here the other day? I'm sure I saw you."

Penny interrupts. "This is not a social call."

"Why are you still on restriction?" Betty asks.

"Were you here?" Karl asks.

"I'm warning you," Penny snaps.

"I'm talking to my wife!" He steps back from Penny and nearly pulls the base of the phone off her desk.

"Why shouldn't I visit, Karl?"

"Because they tell me I have a bad attitude."

"Oh, Karl, you don't want to go back to jail, do you?"

"I want to come home."

Betty says nothing.

"I miss you."

Again silence, except for the sound of Penny tapping her pen against a clipboard. "Just tell her when she can come."

Karl thrusts the receiver at Penny. "You tell her," he says and walks out of the office. There's a traffic jam in the kitchen doorway. House mates Marvin, Kitty, and Lee are planning the night's meal. "Look out," Karl says, pushing through them down the hall and into his room. He slams the door, drops onto his knees and punches the bed until he is breathless.

"I'll fucking go! I'll fucking go! I'll fucking go back to jail!" He screams until he can't lift his arms anymore. He lays his head on the rumpled sheets. He feels hot and cool perspiration breaking on his scalp.

"Fuck it, Betty. You're supposed to be on my side."

****

Cassie has soccer practice after school, and afterward, she'll go to a teammate's house. Betty can't help replaying the previous night's angry remarks in her mind. She had wanted to say: *Do you really think I take out my problems on you? Because I have tried so, so hard...* She had wanted to say, *I'm doing this all on my own. All these years, it's me that worries. It's me...* No, she hadn't wanted to say all that.

Funny, when she dropped Cassie off at school in the morning, she had said, "I love you, Kari." Cassie's head and shoulders were already out of the car. Her attention was on a congregation of girls and boys beside the tether ball pole. She didn't seem to hear the slip.

Betty drives east on River Road toward the home of her brother and sister-in-law in Santa Rosa. The sun has fallen low enough to come up through her back window. The wisps of Ryan's blond hair glow like electric filaments. The man on the radio enumerates U.S. crimes against Haiti over the last two decades. He paints an awful picture of the conditions for political prisoners there. She listens, but new revelations of horror do not produce the old, familiar responses. She clicks off the radio and says, "Life's cheap, Ryan. Life's cheap when you're poor."

"Are we poor?" Ryan asks.

She considers. Subtracting Karl's unreliable income and adjusting for the costs of his bad habits, she doesn't know yet. Will she have him back after he has served his time? She doesn't know yet. She might be able to pick up more hours working at the dental clinic, but then she'll have to spend more on daycare…

"Are we poor, Mommy?" Ryan asks again.

"I guess we have what we need."

"Do we need butterflies in our noses?"

She tilts the rear-view mirror until she finds his self-satisfied smile. "I do, sweetie."

"Do we need tractors in our salad?"

"I do." She reaches between the seats and gives his foot a soft squeeze.

"Do we need–" His head rolls a half turn against the back of his car seat. He's looking dreamily at the passing sky.

"I can tell you're thinking of a good one."

"Do we need daddies in our clouds?"

"I don't know."

She takes Mirabel Road to 116 to Occidental Road, because the highway can be crowded at this hour, and because she likes driving by the marsh where she often sees egrets standing reed-like amid the swamp grass and cattails.

Ryan likes the egrets too. "The long ducks!" Even more, he likes the baler in the next field, spitting out perfect blocks of hay. By the time they come upon the wetlands, Ryan is sleeping. The egrets are where they should be, but they're not so special when she can't share them with him.

In class, Professor McCauley asks the students to read samples of their writing, a page or so. After a brief awkward silence, the woman next to Betty volunteers. She reads a sentimental piece about a family horse with a broken leg. In the story, a girl petitions her father to allow the horse, *aka* Porridge, to live. The father makes a speech about maturity, and the woman reading attempts to capture his voice by dropping her own. Afterward, the professor asks for comments from the class.

A young woman from the back says, "That was so sad. The father seemed really mean, but I believed he would've said that."

Another woman says, "I wanted to see Porridge. I wanted to care about him more."

And another says, "I think I've heard this story before. It might've been interesting to tell it from the horse's point of view." Betty sees the woman beside her cringe. She wants to say something kind, but she had been distracted by the reader's theatrical embellishments and worried that the same might be expected of her.

Next, the seventy-year-old man reads a bizarre story about the founding of Israel. There are no characters, and it doesn't feel like a story at all. Some of the language sounds biblical but nothing that Betty recognizes.

"Thank you," Professor McCauley says. "Who's next?"

Betty turns in her chair. No one is volunteering. She looks at the professor who happens to be looking at her. "Please."

"Well, mine isn't finished," she says.

"That's fine."

"I'll just read a scene."

"Could you speak louder?" the classmate, who had wanted the horse's point of view, asks.

Amber completed her trigonometry problems at the kitchen table and told her mother she's going to bed. Nothing was out of the ordinary, except for the storm brewing inside her belly. Nothing was unusual, except her peculiar resolve, which somehow made everything else, including the tuft in the carpet, the smoothness of the banister, and the long, narrow triangle of light beneath her bedroom door seem brand new. She felt that if she had permitted herself to stop and think, she wouldn't go through with her plan. But was it her *plan? When exactly had* she *decided to sneak out of the house in her sister's clothing?*

She pulls on Kari's skintight, stonewashed hip-huggers and one of her tie-dyed tank tops. She puts on a denim jacket, because Kari had a mole on her left shoulder. She can't wear sandals, because Kari had painted her toenails red and black. She grabs a pair of Doc Martens from under Kari's bed. The finishing touches are the most confusing: the black mascara and silver lip gloss. The mirror shows the fear in her eyes.

She rubs a bar of soap once up and down the tracks, so that the window will slide without squeaking; a trick she had seen Kari do a few times. She cautiously steps through the hole backwards, rests her hands and her waist on the sill, and finds the elm tree's branch with her right boot, then the left. Now, she must blindly push back and catch the branch above her head, which was something she has never had the courage to try before as much as Kari had coaxed and teased her.

What if her mother or father stumbled upon her broken body on the lawn, dressed as her sister only two weeks after her sister's disappearance? It was so horrible to imagine. It was almost funny too. Kari would have found it hysterical. And the fact she – Amber – the cautious one, the good one, can see any humor in it at all is a little bit frightening but exhilarating too. She holds her breath and shoves off into the dark...

****

Penny has several announcements at morning meeting, the last of which is that Karl will receive an extra three days of restriction for rudeness and noncompliance.

He's not surprised, except by the fact that he's not angry. Maybe he had punched out all his anger or sweated it out like some poison, some foul fluid sopped up by his foul-smelling mattress. Is that possible? Something seems to have changed, but maybe it happened in the moments before his private tantrum, when he had said, "come home," and Betty had said nothing.

Karl needs some kind of story to fill that silence. What was it about her seeing him and walking off as if she had not? He can't sit with that. People *do* see red if angry enough, and this feeling of emptiness is real too. He feels loose in the gut with a dull, weakening ache as if his ribcage is expanding or dissolving.

He sits on one of the sofa sectionals surrounded by his alcoholic, drug-addicted housemates. In his civilian life, Karl is a freelance photographer, but he also has a half dozen other jobs: landscaper, house painter, jewelry maker, math tutor, garbage hauler, and wood splitter, because snapping pictures has never paid the bills. He has always hoped his passion and his talent would be recognized, and he would be able to give his full attention to it.

Each morning, Penny has the residents state how they feel, one after another. Karl has consistently muttered *blissful* with a sour expression on his face. Today, when his turn comes, he says, "Okay."

"Just okay?" Penny asks. "That's a change."

"I feel like I've been hollowed out," he explains. "Like someone took a fucking plumber's snake and–"

"Language please," Lee says.

"Sorry."

"Sorry now?" Penny raises her eyebrow. "Another first."

"Hollowed out?" Cherise asks, thoughtfully. "Why do you say that?"

"I don't know where to start." He holds his forehead in the palms of his hands.

"Ask your higher power," Cherise says. "That's what I do."

He shakes his head and closes his eyes. At the suggestion of higher power, he has only ever drawn a blank, but this morning, surprisingly, he conjures up a picture of his father. He can see the old man in his flannel shirt and suspenders. He can almost smell his creosote-soaked dungarees and the pipe. His father had also made a career of odd jobs and had high expectations of himself, but unlike Karl, he didn't give a damn if anyone recognized his abilities. His father, the handyman, the poet, the dope farmer, and the backwoods radical iconoclast, could do any work he set his mind to do. He just couldn't keep a boss. Christ, he'd have a good laugh if he could see his son right now. He'd run his sleeve under his nose and mutter, "Poor bastard."

Karl's stepmother was a little less predictable. She might laugh, scream, spit, or throw a bottle at the wall. In one of her gentler moods, she'd say, "Keep yourself free, honey. Don't be anybody's fool."

****
****

Betty pauses, short of breath, suddenly aware again that she is in a classroom full of people.

"Is there more?" Professor McCauley asks.

"Well, now enters Spike," Betty explains. "He never finished high school. He's nineteen."

"Go on," says McCauley, smiling.

Spike hangs out above the tattoo shop, a one-room apartment on the second floor with no curtains and a bare bulb dangling from the ceiling. But Amber guesses that he'll be steering clear of his old haunts, that while on probation and with the investigation still going, he'll keep his head down and probably stay at his parents' home.

She knows the street, and she thinks she'll find the house by spotting Spike's car parked in front. He has a jacked-up, lemon yellow Le Mans. But she guesses again that the car must've been impounded for evidence. It was, after all, where Kari was last seen. The police had identified her scarf soaked in vomit in the backseat. And, as the report had it, they had found Spike a couple of hundred yards away, shivering, waist deep in the river.

She pulls Kari's jacket tight across her chest and walks three long blocks past hedges, drawn curtains, and flickering blue windows. She looks for any sign of him. She stops and forces her hands deep into the tight pockets of Kari's jeans. A light gust swirls dried oak leaves and bats them against the curb beneath her feet. She hears a young woman's laughter, the scrape of leather boots against concrete, and a man's voice, low and intimate.

She decides to walk on, slowly, three more blocks and then another until the houses give way to the empty drive-through lot of a bank, and she knows that she has gone too far. Turning back, she feels an odd mix of disappointment and relief.

Her plan unravels. But was it hers*? What had she expected to accomplish? Did she really think Spike would be fooled? Did she really think that upon seeing her he'd assume she was Kari or the ghost of Kari? That he'd get down on his knees and plead for mercy? Or that in some other way he'd reveal what happened the night Kari vanished?*

Now Amber can admit to herself the plan was pretty far-fetched pretty goddammed stupid; but what is harder to admit is this driving feeling that she – Amber –absolutely must come face-to-face with the negative influence, the murder suspect, the lover: Spike.

She quits searching left and right, tucks her chin, and pushes forward. She rehearses the quiet reentrance from branch through bedroom window and back to peaceful sleep. She breathes in and out fully for what feels like the first time in hours, maybe days. Oh, to return to her senses.

But there, twenty timorous paces ahead under a dark canopy of trees…

"That's as far as I've gotten," Betty says. "I haven't finished the scene. I don't know what will happen."

"It's creepy," a classmate says. "Kind of like a ghost story."

"I think it's more a love story," another says. "Not the ordinary kind of love story though."

"That business of one twin pretending to be the other. It's so like Patty Duke, you know."

"I just hope Amber gets home safe."

"Thank you," Professor McCauley says. "I'm eager to see where it goes."

Betty blushes like a schoolgirl, and the blushing makes her even more embarrassed.

****

"I don't know anything about god or religion," Karl says. "If that's what you mean by higher power. My folks didn't bring me up to be a joiner. They weren't exactly social."

"I guess it's hard for you to be here," Cherise says.

"Just another sign of failure." He cautions a glance at her and the other faces around the circle.

Lee is nodding slowly as if to the tune of a familiar song.

"Everything's going kind of wide angle on me," Karl says.

"Why don't you say what you mean?" Penny asks.

"I get it," says Cherise. "Like losing perspective."

"Is that right?" asks Penny.

After a long pause, Karl says, "Like if I was to put a camera on you…" He captures Penny in a small frame made by his index fingers and thumbs. She sits with her legs crossed and clipboard balanced on her knee. "Then I'd want to separate you from what surrounds you. Marvin there, Kitty, and that chair. See what I'm saying? I'd want you to stand out."

Penny uncrosses and re-crosses her legs. Her eyes show only suspicion. "I don't like metaphors," she says. "I like it when people say what they mean."

Karl peels his fingers apart, keeping his eyes focused on Penny. "Maybe you don't like the feeling that you blend in with the background. "The way I'm feeling now."

"You don't like it," Cherise agrees.

"I'm tired of fighting it," he says. "I don't know if I can anymore."

"Well," Penny says, "sounds a little like humility. It's an important first step. But I have my doubts."

"I only know I miss my wife, my girl, and my little boy."

"Maybe you should have thought of them before getting behind the wheel drunk and putting your girl in danger."

Karl doesn't have the strength or desire to defend himself. There were extenuating circumstances, but no one has ever wanted to hear them. He lets his head fall into his hands again. "Fuck. Sorry."

****

Betty expects Mr. Roberts at ten o'clock for a full cleaning, but he cancels ten minutes before his appointment. She doesn't have another on the schedule for an hour and a half. She takes out her notebook and pen, sits in a big reclining chair, and looks up at one of the posted pictures of a perfect set of teeth.

Spike had gotten his hair cut short and shaved the fuzz off his chin. He seems younger. He seems older? He is handsome. But is he drunk? He is with a young woman. He is walking with his mother, elbow in elbow. He needs to floss...

"I've got to get the hell out of here," Betty announces to no one.

Passing the front desk, she tells the receptionist that she'll be back in time for her eleven thirty. She heads west on 116 through Guerneville to Duncan's Mills, where the coffee is strong, and the sky seems huge, unobstructed by redwood trees.

A voice on the radio urges, "We need your support to continue bringing you this kind of programming..." She clicks it off. There was nothing new on the CIA leak story, except that Cheney appointed two checkered characters to fill Libby's post.

Bush nominated another Supreme Court Justice. Rosa Parks died. It surprises Betty that Rosa Parks hadn't died way back when. She seems part of another era, another lifetime.

The last time Betty saw Mr. Roberts for his 'spring cleaning,' he had made a remark about her choice of radio station. Later, her boss -- the gray ponytailed, surfer, vegan, Chris Chesney DDS -- had told her to find something closer to the center of the dial. Seems funny now but she was livid at the time. She had rehearsed a speech but then swallowed hard and given in without a fight. Without even a single word.

Soon after, she stopped liking her job. She had chosen not to tell Karl about it. She knew he would've been angry, and he might have scolded her for being such a coward. But on this front, he would've been her ally.

She sits at a picnic table with her notebook open and a double iced espresso. For forty minutes, she watches the big sky turn nervous. *Do we need daddies in our clouds?* Will she have Karl back in her life, and if so, under what circumstances?

She simply hasn't wanted to think about it, and she has told herself many times that she doesn't have to, not yet.

What does Amber really want from Spike?

In the real story all those years ago, the reckless daughter returned. For all the nightly news drama, the celebration was short-lived. One rumor had it that the girl had gotten pregnant and left the state to get an abortion. Another said that she had dropped acid and had a psychotic break. In any case, the story ended abruptly, disappearing from the screen soon after the family moved away. Little was ever said about the well-behaved twin. *Why does Amber need to confront Spike?* Betty bites down on her lower lip.

She glances at her watch and gasps. She packs up and heads back to work. "Because if Amber doesn't, Professor McCauley will know what a chicken shit I am."

****
****

At 6 p.m., the day's meetings are finished, dinner is over, and most of the chores are done. Those who aren't on 10 Day Freeze or some other form of restriction typically walk a few blocks to an AA meeting and go out for coffee afterward. Karl must stay home though. He's forbidden to watch TV, and he's bored with the paperback novels he brought with him when he moved in.

Cherise decided to skip AA tonight because, she said she had some packing to do. They convene on a bench beside the vegetable garden. He has cigarettes, and she has a match.

"You must be feeling pretty good," he says. "What? Two more days here?"

"I'm pretty scared I'd say."

"Yeah," he says. "Not so sure what you're getting back into."

She smiles. "Or who I'll be."

It strikes Karl that she's not quite who he thought she was. He had assumed that all his fellow residents had been hypnotized by Penny, but Cherise seems to have her own mind. He whispers, as if to himself, "Change the lens; change the picture."

"Hmm." She blows out smoke and throws her hair over one shoulder. "I've been thinking about mirrors," she says. "How you can see your own reflection in everything, in everyone." She smiles.

Karl nods. "Got a family?"

"Just a boyfriend."

"He drinks too?"

"Oh yeah." She laughs. "He loves his tequila and beer."

"How's that going to be?"

She stares at the side of the house as if maybe she hasn't heard him or as if she's straining to hear something else. The only sound comes from her bedroom window, a tiny clock radio. After a long pause, "I don't want to go back to the way things were," she says. "What about you?"

Karl laughs. "Ask me in three months."

"Yeah."

"Right now, I'd kill for a glass of whiskey."

"You're just starting out. That's normal."

"I'm glad to hear something's normal," he says. "Shit."

Cherise stubs out her smoke, stands, and stretches her arms over her head.

He feels a sudden desire to put his hands on her waist and pull her to him. He looks away. "Something is in the air," he says. "I feel… I don't know."

She smiles. "I guess I'd better get back to my packing."

"I'd better get back to my whatever," he says.

She laughs. "You know," she says from halfway across the lawn, "Penny shouldn't have said what she said. You'll make it through the program. You will if you want to."

He sits on the picnic table, examining his toes through the tops of his sandals. *Higher power?* He had been told that it doesn't have to be God. It can be anything you want it to be. Karl's father had once described himself as an anarcho-syndicalist. He called his philosophy 'principled skepticism.' And yes, Karl admired his old man's independence and self-assurance. Surely, he had inherited his dad's posture and at least a little bit of the surliness, at least some of the time. He had learned at a young age to associate real power with freethinking and freethinking with political activism. He had spent more than a dozen nights in jail with friends, and for causes he believed in, in most cases. Higher power, as he has understood it, is invariably something to be resisted, rebelled against.

In the years after his stepmother left with a real estate salesman, Karl had seen his father turn bitter. The old man wasn't taking life on his own terms, he was merely reacting, a creature of habit like anyone else. To think of him alone in his cabin in Cazadero, smoking fatties and reading the same obscure essays about the Kronstadt Rebellion or Haymarket Square he'd read twenty years ago, he really had become a caricature of himself.

The highest power Karl had ever known was the feeling he'd had when he fell in love with Betty -- the feeling that she loved him. The power was *in* him then. God, was it fourteen years ago? It was mid-October, as it was now, with the same sweet scent of rotting leaves.

Karl had first seen her at the one and only coffee shop in Duncan's Mills, where a dozen of his photos was mounted on the wall. He was a regular and did some jobs now and then for the owner. Betty was passing through and foolish enough to order the rum Danish, a three-day-old almond croissant recycled with a healthy dousing of booze to cover the taste of the mold. He watched her pick it apart and taste it slowly, thoughtfully as if it were some sort of delicacy. He didn't think, *stupid-ass tourist*, as he had often thought when he saw a new face in town. He felt the strange desire to put his hand on hers, if only to make her stop eating that thing.

He watched as Betty circled something in the newspaper and then paused to turn her ballpoint over in her fingers. When she lifted her eyes, she couldn't help but see him studying her.

She blushed. She looked back at her paper, toyed with the handle of her coffee cup, and picked at her pastry. She was like a bad actor trying to look busy. To think of her trying twice, three times to swallow that little bite of Danish; he hadn't meant to make her feel uncomfortable, but he couldn't have taken his eyes off her if he'd wanted to. She stood to examine the photos on the wall, *anything*, he was sure, to turn her back on him.

"It's called 'River Life,'" Karl said, standing two feet behind her.

"You did these?" Her voice seemed trapped and small. She cleared her throat and tried again. "These are your pictures?"

"Those are some of my friends," he said. "They camp out year-round. I guess you'd call them homeless, but they don't think of it that way."

"Reminds me of…" Betty bit her finger.

"Walker Evans," Karl said. "One of my heroes."

"His pictures told stories," she said and laughed. "What do I know? I took one elective in college." She stepped closer to a black and white picture of a woman hanging laundry on a rope between two bay trees. The woman wore tattered sweatpants, a soiled vest, and a bandanna on her head. Behind her was a bedroll and a small fire pit made of bricks and stones. She had pretty eyes and a masculine jaw; she was smiling as if she had just heard something amusing. She clearly enjoyed the attention of the man with the camera.

"She calls herself Ma Kettle." Karl laughed. "She's only twenty-eight."

"Can't be an easy life."

"Summer isn't bad," he said, "except for the tourists and the cops. But most of the year it's damp and cold. You've got to have a strong constitution."

"You admire her." When Betty turned and looked at his face, he was stunned. She was vibrating, ever so slightly, like human fluorescence.

"I do," Karl said. "I admire people who make their own way."

"That's what I'm trying to do," she said. "I'm a tourist, but not for long, I hope." She put her hand out to shake and introduce herself. It was soft and small, but her grip was firm. He could tell she didn't ordinarily talk to strangers and what he was experiencing – the pulse that traveled through his fingers – was the first hint of her resolve. He held onto her hand and pulled her to the next picture.

"This old guy," he said, pointing, "is an original Wobbly. He can tell some stories, but he's the crankiest bastard you'd ever want to meet."

Betty swallowed. "I'd like to meet him."

And so, it began. She'd rushed off to get a sweater from the seat of her VW bus. As he watched her return, he was stunned by her peculiar walk, hurry and hesitation, effort and grace. Uncertainty, even fear made perfect sense under the circumstances; she was about to take a ride with a strange man, and probably far from home. He had known plenty of indecisive, muddle-headed people, but she wasn't like them at all. She was animated by her ambivalence.

Betty straddled the back of Karl's motorcycle and pressed her pink fists into his coat pockets as they rode to the camp of the grouchiest man alive. They made a quick stop for a tin of chew and a pint of blackberry brandy.

"The cost of admission," Karl explained. And when they arrived, their unsuspecting host was not at home. "Probably off to score dope in Monte Rio," Karl said.

"Well now, what are we going to do with all this brandy?" She smiled. She brushed off a wide stump and invited him to sit beside her. And so, it began, Karl and Betty told their dreams and shared the highlight reels of their lives so far, each culminating in this moment, just a stone's throw from the muddy river.

Karl remembers it in warm summer light, but it couldn't have been that way. His memory always betrays him these days. His thoughts are interrupted by Cherise calling from her window.

"Hey! Did you hear? Rosa Parks died."

****

No, Betty says to herself as she drives east on River Road, the big sky falling away behind her. She hadn't come to Duncan's Mills to think about Karl or the early days of their relationship; but perhaps she had come to think about herself, the young woman with the camper bus who was fresh out of grad school, cruising down the coast all the way from the Olympic Peninsula with her future just beyond her front bumper. What a good and sensible girl she had been – patriotic, law-abiding, unassuming, and unquestioning. She was a budding dental hygienist and a daughter to make her Wyoming-bred, Republican parents proud. Except for her road trip, she had always done what was expected of her. But even the trip was expected. It was the time in a life when a young woman sees the big world, broadens a little, gets frightened and lonely, and gets *it* out of her system. Everything had been going as planned, though it wasn't as Betty planned.

No, that's not what she had come to think about either, not intentionally. She had come out from under the shadows of the tall trees for a fresh perspective, to discover what Amber will do. She shouldn't have left Amber in such a predicament. She is too young, too good. She should be mourning the disappearance of her sister, not trying to become like her.

Passing back through Guerneville, she sees two girls and a boy walking along the side of the road toward the center of town. *They should be in school*, she thinks. They shouldn't be smoking, those tender pink lungs. Those gums. Wait. That's Cassie's striped running jacket. That's Cassie!

The girlfriend Betty knows is not from the soccer team, and she can't remember having seen her at school. She saw her only once, a face that had seemed to materialize out of the darkness the night Karl was arrested. The girl wears a heavy coat of mascara, looks owlish and a little old for high school. The boy is not familiar at all, though that night, she had felt vaguely aware of another presence, someone or something beckoning from a shadowy somewhere. What a confusing, awful night that was.

Betty stops her car in front of Lark's Drug's, across the street from the Rainbow Cattle Company, which was the scene of all that awfulness. She's not angry. Not yet. Not even when she sees Cassie at the corner of the plaza, putting her friend's long filtered cigarette to her lips. It's not funny either, though it could be – the utter concentration in the gesture as if Cassie would miss her mouth if she weren't trying so hard.

As she sits in her car, the night comes back to her, and with it a pain in her gut.

Karl had said that he needed to meet someone about a possible job. "A magazine editor," he said with enthusiasm. The job was landscaping, but Karl was excited to make a new connection, and surely, he was hoping for a chance to publish his new series of photos, *Campesinos in the Vineyards*. He had been unusually buoyant. He had been drinking even though he denied it. Karl's license had been suspended for DUI just ten months before.

That cold, rainy late afternoon drizzled into evening. Karl had promised he'd be back soon enough to help put the kids to bed. But Betty was left to do the full routine alone again for the fourth night in a row: Ryan wound way up before winding down and Cassie was in extreme sulk mode over who knows what. There was no milk for the bedtime hot chocolate. Ryan was in his pajama top, naked below the waist and hiding behind the sofa. She shoved the sofa out of her way and heaved him up on her shoulder. His little fists swung. She ordered Cassie to get in the car, and they headed for the grocery store. Her head pulsed with rage. There – here now – in front of The Rainbow Cattle Company was Karl's pickup; her suspicions confirmed.

She'd stopped, double-parked. "Wait right here."

"Wait! Here? Not with this screaming nut job!" Cassie hollered.

"You better," she said, pointing her finger at the wrinkle between Cassie's eyes. "You better." But all the threats that came to mind she had intended for Karl. She slammed her door and charged, slipping and almost falling on the wet pavement and into the saloon. Just inside, she was greeted by the sharp smell of stale beer, the shrill guitar of B.B. King on the juke box, and darkness, except for a string of pin-sized red Christmas lights over the bar.

"Betty? Bet? Is everything okay?"

She saw Karl ten feet away, seated beside no editor but instead a spiky-haired, leather-clad lesbian, one of the local realtors on her favorite piece of real estate. She watched Karl push himself back from the bar with his half-filled glass of whiskey.

"I just needed to see for myself," she said. Having said so, it felt true. Her rage, that wonderful, horrible energy rippling through her sinews, seemed to have spent itself. "Don't bother coming home, Karl."

"Betty, wait," he said. He stepped toward her.

The bartender, a burly man in a black vest, offered her a shrug and a sheepish grin. The dozen or so patrons had turned their attention back to their cocktails and conversations. She had half turned to go. The car was badly parked, and her children were in their own uproar.

Karl drew nearer with his earnest face and conciliatory tone. His hand loomed larger. She did not want him to touch her. She didn't want to hear apologies or explanations of any kind. Yet, she paused.

What dawned on her then was as disheartening as anything she'd ever experienced – she was merely the counterpart, the leading lady in this alcoholic drama. In spite of all his high ideals and her high hopes, this banal scene had been scripted for them years ago. For fuck's sake, the other men and women at their stools knew exactly what was happening, and it bored them. She smacked his hand away and exited the bar as forcefully as she had entered.

He followed.

Betty and Karl were then briefly frozen in place just outside the doorway, illuminated by the pulsing blue light of a cruiser parked across the street. Karl put his head down. He moved quickly, but it appeared slow with the strobe effect. He lifted bare-assed, wailing Ryan out of the backseat of Betty's car, and he hugged the boy tight to his chest. Betty stood with her hands in the air, helpless and confused.

She turned and saw Cassie halfway down the block by the entrance to the video store, talking to the owlish girl. She seemed oblivious to the unfolding scene. Her hands were in her coat pockets, and her full attention was on her friend, who had apparently said something hilarious. Cassie bent over laughing.

Betty bore down on them with her rage returning, doubling with each step. She had never hit anyone ever, but she slapped Cassie hard across the face.

What exactly did the officer witness? Betty still doesn't know for certain, only that he had chosen to wait in his cruiser and let the scene unfold.

She swept Ryan out of Karl's arms and put him back in his car seat. Karl whispered something; she didn't want to hear. Cassie refused to get back into Betty's car. So, Betty drove away. She forgot to buy milk.

An hour later, the sheriff brought Cassie home with the following news: "Your husband is in jail. He has been arrested for driving on a suspended license and reckless endangerment."

The light changes, and the driver behind Betty taps her horn. She rolls forward slowly.

Cassie's girlfriend ashes out her cigarette on a cement wall. The boy points in the direction of the bridge. The girl points the opposite way, possibly back to school.

Betty steals a glance at her watch. Even if she had another minute to spare, she doesn't know what she'd say or do. She thinks she can see the look on Cassie's face if she were to approach. She pictures Cassie walking away from her again, and it gives her a shudder.

****
****

At 11:30 p.m., Tim, the night counselor, has poked his flashlight inside each of the bedrooms and retired into the office. Lee snores like a mud-soaked whistle. Karl rises from bed, fully dressed, takes his sandals in his hand, and slips down a short corridor to the door. Once he crosses the lot and steps beyond the picket fence, he is officially AWOL. If he's caught, he'll be taken back to jail. So be it.

The day had been cold and dark and wet.

The only brightness, Cherise, has now moved on.

Karl had been accused and convicted of bringing the mail from the box on the front porch to the office door, a job belonging exclusively to staff. He had been told to write an essay about the importance of adhering to house rules. The length of his required essay was promptly doubled from three to six pages, because he said, "You can't be fucking serious." A grown man shouldn't have to live like this – one stupid humiliation after another.

His father wouldn't put up with it. His stepmother wouldn't. Nor would Emma Goldman.

At the time of admission into the program, he was permitted to keep the change in his pocket -- three dollars and ninety-six cents. Or more likely, it was an oversight. All his other possessions had been inventoried. His cash had been locked in a box in the office. Under the circumstances, in what he perceived as a climate of distrust, he felt no need or desire to be forthcoming with his last nickels.

He walks down E Street toward a convenience store. The damp fog of the late afternoon has cleared, and the bristling air puts tears in his eyes. A simple crime, he realizes, is really a complex series of choices. There are many crimes and many opportunities to turn back. If he *is* an addict as they tell him he is, then he is choosing to be so now and now and now. Or is this choice only an illusion? It seems as if the experts want to have it both ways, but where does that leave him? If his behavior is only the manifestation of his illness, why should he feel responsible? Why should he feel guilty? But where is the dignity in that line of thinking?

The thoughts are persistent and wearying. All he wants is a little clarity, and a chance to feel good for a change. He wants to leap over this moment to the next.

"Hey," says a man sitting on the curb.

"Hey."

"Better watch yourself." The man rises unsteadily to his feet. He pats the pockets of his worn coat. "Lots of punks around here."

"Really?" Karl doesn't see anyone.

"Got a cigarette?"

Karl holds out a Camel Light, and the man nearly falls into him when he reaches for it. Beneath the man's whiskers are a dozen scabs from his chin to his right ear. "Got a match?"

When Karl steps closer, he is overcome by the smell of shit. He tries to hide his revulsion, but the man isn't looking at Karl's face anyway. "Got a couple of bucks you can spare?"

"Not this time," Karl says.

"My ass is about froze off."

"Sorry." Karl backs away. His hands are in the air as if to say there's nothing he can do. When he turns, he can see the blue and white electric Pepsi sign above his oasis. He wills his hands into his pockets, wills his way backward through the glass door, and wills… *Enough already.*

He steps up to the register and asks for the cheapest vodka on the shelf. He sets his change on the counter. He has fifty cents to spare. When he exits the store, is it will or the felt absence of it that guides him to the pay phone?

She won't be up, but she might get up. He is relieved to hear his name still included on the family message. His hand is shaking. The cold receiver shakes against his ear. He waits.

"Hello?"

"Betty."

"Oh no. Karl, where are you?"

"Betty."

"You need to go right back to that group home."

"Yes," he says. "Yes, honey. I know."

"Right away! Before anyone knows you're gone."

"Yes," he says, but the sound is trapped inside his throat.

"I'm going to call there, Karl. I'm going to ask for you. Fifteen minutes."

Weeping comes over him like a convulsion.

"Karl?"

"I just need..."

"What, Karl? What is it?"

"I just needed..."

"Karl?"

"Your voice."

"I know, honey. I know."

He puts the receiver back in its cradle. Several paces ahead, he hands off his brown paper package to the man on the curb. "Merry Christmas."

****
****

Betty can't go back to sleep. She doesn't want to laugh, and she really, *really* doesn't want to cry. No popcorn. No TV. She might like to write if she could see her way through Amber's predicament. If she had a clearer sense of what she'd like to have happen. When she had started, it was fun, something new to think about. It was as if the scenes were appearing before her eyes, and she couldn't scribble fast enough, but now it's all become opaque and oppressive.

She doesn't want to be alone, but who would she call? She can't help thinking of Karl, one of his familiar tirades.

"We're all scared shitless of one another," he often said. "That's capitalism and the corporate media at work. Your neighbors are arsonists, pedophiles, and serial killers. Stay in and play with your toys. Buy bigger and better. If you need company, watch Seinfeld or Cheers. Watch Friends!"

All her friends were his friends, and where are they now? She doesn't want to be alone.

Comes a pair of feet that look like small flippers with the socks sliding down so. Here come hands pushing through a curtain, a mop of blond hair, and eyes squinting against the kitchen light.

"Did the phone wake you up, sweetie?"

She doesn't expect an answer. She sweeps Ryan in her arms and carries him to the sofa. They snuggle under a blanket, and she enjoys the warmth of him. Now, she hears the creak of a wooden ladder; Cassie descends from her loft bed.

"What's going on?" Cassie asks, knuckles pressed deep into her eyes.

"Your father called."

"Oh my god. How is he?"

Betty lifts the blanket and makes space for Cassie beside her.

Cassie sits.

"I don't know," she says. She puts an arm around Cassie's shoulders, and with her fingers, she gently examines her long hair. "He misses us."

"I miss him, too."

"I thought you did. You haven't said a word about it though."

"I didn't want to say it to you," Cassie says.

They sit quietly for two minutes, staring at the black TV. Cassie's words have made Betty sadder but also relieved. *At least she feels she can tell me now.*

Cassie leans forward and says, "Looks like nuthead went back to sleep."

"I know. I could feel it."

"Your weight changes when you die," Cassie says. "It's like your soul is leaving your body or something."

"I've heard that, but it has never been proven," Betty says.

"Mrs. Robinson said it in class."

"Since when do you listen to your teachers?"

"I just think it's true."

"Do you think smoking cigarettes is bad for you?" Betty asks in a mildly inquisitive tone.

"I don't know," Cassie says.

Betty feels her pull away, just an inch, but tensely. She pulls Cassie back and squeezes. She thinks, *I've never been as old as I am right now. My daughter has never been this old. Every moment between us is a frontier, a cliff.* "You know. You know plenty."

They sit quietly for another minute.

"Mom?"

"What?"

"Never mind."

"I'm going to put nuthead in his bed," Betty says.

"Are you going to visit Dad tomorrow?"

"If he's not in some kind of trouble."

"Can I come with you?"

"I was hoping you would."

The class is debating the merits of good taste vs. the need for verisimilitude. Would the rapist *really* have said, "I'm going to do you"? Or "Yeah baby, I'm doing you now"? Would the victim have said, "Stop doing me"?

To make matters worse, the author insists that that's how it really happened.

McCauley signals timeout with his hands. "It doesn't matter what really happened," he says. "The story makes its own demands."

Betty copies his remark in her notebook.

"Do you have something new for us?" McCauley asks her.

Betty clears her throat.

Amber steps off the sidewalk, through a gap in a hedge, and onto someone's front lawn. She can see a man's silhouette in the light of a streetlamp filtered through the bare branches of an overhanging elm. It's Spike all right: broad shoulders, trim waist, and baggy pants. He has not shaved the fuzz off his chin. He stops walking to light a cigarette. He takes two steps and stops again. "Is someone there?"

Amber shuffles backward and brushes the head of a shovel with her foot. She catches the handle before it falls and pulls it tight against her chest.

"Is someone there?" he asks again.

"Someone's here, Spike," she says.

"Who are you?"

She steps out onto the sidewalk and into the dim light. She can't read the expression on his face, but she can hear anguish in his voice. "This isn't funny," he says. "Who are you?"

"You can't hurt me, Spike," she says. "Not again."

He steps forward abruptly.

She waves the shovel like a spear.

"Amber," he says. "You're freaking me out."

"How do you know I'm Amber?" she asks.

"Because…"

"How *do you know?"*

He looks down at his feet.

Amber feels her knees go weak. Now what? "How do you know? How do you know I'm not her?" she demands.

He sighs, shakes his head, and tugs at the hair on his chin. "Okay, okay. I get it. If I had an identical twin, I'd probably try to pull some Patty Duke bullshit too."

She raises the shovel and aims the point at his throat...

****

Can Karl remember having a functioning memory? It seems to function somewhat differently lately. He has been told that a part of his condition is denial of the condition.

So, what if he stops denying it? What if he embraces it instead? He still doesn't know what's fucking real and what's not.

Once late at night, not so long ago, he had been standing on his front lawn barefoot, and Betty had locked the door. He had to come in through a window. He scraped the top of his head and fell asleep on the couch.

Once, he had called her a cunt, or she had said he had. Did she ever remember the names she called him? Did she ever apologize? Many times, he'd wanted to have a family picnic at the coast or a hike through the redwoods up to Bullfrog Pond, but she wouldn't. His wants were always frivolous or selfish even when they were not. Once, his head was in her lap while she examined the scrape on his scalp. He was crying.

Did he betray her? Did she betray him? Or is there a third alternative where they both were betrayed by some middle-class fantasy of happiness? Is all their suffering and discord the result of diminished desire? Failed imagination? False consciousness? One thing is certain: she believed in him, and now she doesn't.

"I want to congratulate Karl," Penny announced at morning meeting. "He is finally off restriction."

"Way to go, Karl!"

"Good going, man."

And another thing's for sure: he has stopped believing in himself. Is it necessary to go back, strip off the covers as they say, identify the misunderstandings and the lies? Is it even possible?

"I'm so happy for you, Karl."

"Thanks," he says, flatly. And because there seems to be an expectation for more, he adds, "I'm tired."

****
****

They're driving east on River Road. Betty and Cassie in the front, and Ryan is in his car seat in the back. It is midafternoon. The last traces of fog have evaporated, and the sky is clear blue above the golden vineyards.

The kids are clean and well-combed. It's funny, because Betty is reminded of her childhood in Wyoming. She and her parents would be in their church clothes, driving across the county to visit Grandma. Oh, such energy and attention given to making a respectable appearance. It's funny how after so many years and so many changes, a certain few defining images of *family* persist.

Try now to picture Cassie in a homemade, knee-length dress. Try to picture Karl at the wheel in a coat and tie. Now, that's funny.

Betty didn't sleep well last night or the night before. "We can't stay long with Daddy, you know."

"I know," Cassie says.

"I know," Ryan repeats. "Why?"

"Because I have to go to class, and you have to go to your aunt and uncle's."

"Can Daddy come?" Ryan asks.

"No, but we can come see him again on Sunday." Under her breath, Betty adds, "If he behaves himself."

"I don't think you should say things like that," Cassie says.

"Maybe I should keep it to myself."

"Does Daddy have behavior?" Ryan asks.

"You bet he does."

Cassie leans forward and turns up the radio. "Sounds like the man is talking about Rosa Parks."

"That's Jesse Jackson," Betty says. "Your father and I saw him speak in Washington D.C. years ago. We sat on a huge lawn with thousands of other people. It was our honeymoon." She laughs. "Or that's what we called it."

"And Daddy was arrested, right?"

"Not that time, but he spent plenty of nights in jail. I got locked up a few times myself before you were born."

"Really?"

"We had high hopes," Betty says. "Long ago."

"We've been hearing about Rosa Parks in school," Cassie says. "I don't get it. I mean, she wouldn't give up her seat on a bus. Why is that such a big deal?"

"It took courage," Betty says.

"I guess," Cassie says, "but lots of people have courage, don't they?"

As Betty turns onto E Street, two blocks from the group home, she suddenly feels unprepared. She swallows hard. Why hadn't she thought this all the way through? Why hadn't she come up with a plan? With an unhelpful rush of adrenaline, she leans forward as if to listen closely to the radio, but all she can hear is blood beating in her ears. "You should ask your father."

Betty pulls the car to curbside. She examines her face in the rear-view mirror.

Cassie unbuckles her seat belt and waits for her mother to open her door before she releases the latch on her own.

Ryan announces, "I have to pee."

Cassie frees Ryan from his car seat as Betty retrieves a box of cigarettes and a small tin of foot powder from the trunk.

Penny, with her jangling keys, happens to be crossing the lot and greets Betty at the picket fence. "I see you've brought your children."

"Yes."

"That's a bit of a surprise. We don't often have children visit."

Betty nods, barely.

Penny stands between Betty and the entrance to the group home. She smiles long and hard at Cassie and then Ryan.

Betty says, "Ryan has to use the bathroom."

"Follow me," Penny says. "All visitors have to sign in. And it looks like you've brought some things for Karl. I'll have to check those out."

Betty can feel Cassie's curious glance like a jet of hot air against her cheek. Her face is set, her neck and shoulders rigid; it's as if her body has decided to prepare for a roller coaster ride. She is not certain what she is afraid of, but she doesn't like the scrutiny nor the assumptions she knows have been made about her. Maybe there's meth in the foot powder! Is that what they think?

Cassie whispers, "What's wrong, Mom?"

"Nothing. What do you mean?"

"You could chill out a little. That's all."

Ryan runs through the open door to a large metal cabinet with file folders and boxes of medicine in bubble packs. "Is this Daddy's new house?" he asks.

"This is the office," Penny says. "Not a place for children."

Marvin appears behind Betty and looks over her shoulder into the office.

"You can see I'm busy, can't you?" Penny snaps. "If you want to do something useful, let Karl know that his family is here."

Marvin backs away expressionless or almost so. Betty spies a hint of embarrassment. She thinks, *there is a man who has swallowed his pride so often that he barely knows the taste of it.*

Karl appears. His hair is wet. "I was in the--" he says. "You're here. I was just in the shower." He pulls a chair away from the kitchen table and then slides it back again. "I wasn't sure you were coming."

"Hi Daddy," Ryan says. He runs through the office doorway and hugs Karl's knee. "Is this your new house? Can we live here too?"

Karl bends low and wraps his arms around Ryan, but only briefly because Ryan squirms loose and runs down a corridor, searching.

"Hi Dad." Cassie gives her father a long hug. "You shaved your sideburns."

"I did."

"You look so much younger."

"Do I?" Karl is looking over the top of Cassie's head at Betty in the office doorway.

Betty averts her eyes, studying her cuticles.

"Come with me?" Karl asks her.

"Living room or picnic table," Penny calls from the office.

"I know," Karl says.

"House rules," Penny continues. "Not in the bedroom."

"I *know.*"

"What do you think we're going to do?" Betty asks. "Fuck in front of the children?"

Karl looks at Betty, stunned.

"God, Mom," Cassie moans. "I can't believe you just said that."

Betty asks Karl for a cigarette.

"You don't smoke, Mom," Cassie says.

"Go look after your brother," she says.

Karl and Betty step outside onto a porch. With trembling hands, he produces one of his Camel Lights.

"I can't stand it, Karl. I don't want to be here."

"I know," he says. "Neither do I."

"I don't know what I want," she says. "I try to know, but I can't."

He reaches for her hand, but she pulls back.

"Can you accept that?" she asks.

Cautiously, he embraces her, pulling her to him. "Do I have a choice?"

* * *

Cassie walks down a corridor, searching for Ryan. She finds him alone in the living room with a TV remote in his hand. He clicks rapidly through the channels. Even though she sees a program she'd like to watch, she knows it'd be too much work to persuade him.

* * *

Out on the porch, Karl feels self-conscious holding Betty, because she is straight and as firm as a plank. He holds her anyway. He whispers, "I only wish I could have seen Penny's face when you–"

"You should've seen *your* face."

They laugh.

* * *

When Cassie attempts to grab the remote from Ryan, he tosses it against a wall, and it falls behind one of the sofa sectionals. A small piece of plastic came loose from the back, and she can't find the batteries. They are stuck with C-SPAN, a White House press conference, the head and shoulders of Scott McClellan above a podium.

Cassie throws up her hands, and walks outside, where she sees her mother and father sitting opposite one another. Karl is bent forward with his hands in the center of a picnic table, face tilted down. Betty's hands are fastened to the edge of the table as if she might fall if she let go.

"Dad," Cassie says. "Mom said I should ask you about Rosa Parks."

"What about her? She was very brave."

"Mom said that too, but a lot of people are brave."

"She was a fulcrum."

"I don't think that's a word Cassie knows," Betty says.

"It's like the lever on a machine that makes it go. It's like there was this great big machine – a social justice machine – all fueled up and ready; it just needed to be turned on."

"Huh?" Cassie asks.

"There's no question that she was brave," Betty says. "Who knew what those cops might have done to her."

"It wasn't just courage though," Karl says.

"Or what some angry bigot might have done to her family," Betty adds. One of her hands rises from the edge of the table and gathers the fabric of her collar. "I remember the pictures. That frail little woman and those big men…"

"The pictures were important," Karl says. "People doubt what they read and hear, but pictures don't lie."

Cassie nods, but there is still a wrinkle in her brow.

"She was like a picture of dignity."

"What's dignity?"

Karl looks at Cassie and then at Betty. One of his hands turns, palm up. He swallows. "I guess I thought I knew," he says, "but I'm still learning."

* * *

North on Mendocino and west on Third, she has left Karl alone with his thoughts and his torment. Now, she leaves the kids at her brother and sister-in-law's. Their aunt greets them with kisses in the driveway. Their uncle stands in the door, smiling. The kids seem relieved to be out of the car.

Cassie starts walking towards the house, but she turns around and leans into Betty's window. "I think it's going to be okay, Mom."

Betty's eyes are thick and shimmering. She wipes them with her sleeve and nods.

Back to Mendocino and north past College, they're rattling the sabers again; it's Iran this time. It's time for that hundredth monkey to show up and past time for Betty to make some big decisions. She finds parking on a side street. In class, there is only remaining seat in the front row.

McCauley smiles when he sees her. He asks her to share what she has.

Spike doesn't flinch. His eyes slowly rise from the head of the shovel to Amber's face. He looks neither frightened nor angry. He looks weary. He says in a voice drained of conviction, "I guess if I had lost my sister, I'd want to kill the person I thought was responsible."

Amber hasn't got a clue what to say or what direction she'd like this – this thing – to go in.

"I'm going to sit on the curb. If you want, you can knock me over the head with your shovel." He sits. "Or you can sit next to me, and we can talk."

She doesn't swing the shovel. She doesn't sit. She can't move.

"You might not believe this," he says. "Kari wanted to be like you, but she couldn't. She could never be that good."

"You don't know me, Spike."

"I guess I don't," he says. "I only know what Kari said about you. She talked about you all the time."

"Yeah right. What'd she say about me?"

"She said you're naturally responsible. You always do the right thing, because it makes you feel good."

"Bullshit," Amber mutters. "I'm so tired of–"

"She couldn't be like you, so she had to be different. As different as she could be."

"She was just fine Spike until you came along."

"No," he says. "Of all people, you should know that she wasn't fine. She felt like a failure. She told me that she could never measure up, and she was sick of trying."

"That's why she took drugs! That's why she ran into the river! Is that what you're saying? Are you saying it was all my fault?"

"It was her fault. I only blame you for not telling her."

"Telling her what?"

"That you missed her. That you loved her." He sighs again, heavily this time. "I blame myself too. Every day. Every night."

She stands in place until the shovel in her hands feels like the weight of the world. Until it drops with a clang onto the pavement. A fraction of a second later, Amber falls.

Is this what fainting feels like? It can't be.

She thinks she hears Spike scrambling to his feet. She thinks she hears him holler, "No, Amber!" She thinks she sees his face contorted in pain, inches from her own. If she is conscious, it is a different kind of consciousness than any she has ever experienced. She feels as if she has passed through a window into some other realm, and she has left her body behind.

One of his hands falls upon her shoulder, and the other brushes her cheek. She cannot move to resist him. If resisting him is what she wants to do. Her thoughts come rapidly, and she tries to speak, but she cannot hear her own words.

She might have said, "Did you love her, Spike? Did you kill her? Why?" Or as she imagined herself floating back through the window with his warm hand bracing the side of her face, she might have said, "Tell me, Spike. Please. How can we go on?"

In the end, all she can be sure of was that he lifted her off the ground and carried her home.

Oh. And his unsatisfactory response: "My lawyer told me not to answer any questions."

Betty closes her notebook. She sighs. It has been a long, draining day, and nothing seems clearer. She'll try again with Karl because she knows too well how to live without faith.

Because she thinks it's better to believe him and be wrong than not to believe him.

How can we go on? Stubbornly. With dignity. With hope. They'll go on like Rosa Parks did. Exhausted. Uncertain. One ordinary act of courage after another.

She waits for the groans and protests of her classmates to subside before she says, "I know. I'm sorry. I have trouble with endings."

CPSIA information can be obtained
at www.ICGtesting.com
Printed in the USA
FSHW021127140222
88230FS